"Here," she said. She took her finger and swirled it around the inside of the coconut, then placed her fingers to my lips. I surprised myself by sucking hungrily. My eyes were closed; I was intent on drawing out every ounce of succulent moisture from her fingertips. When I opened my eyes, I was shocked to see that she had inserted her breast into the open coconut, and when she removed it, it too was laced and dripping with white.

Obediently, I moved my lips to her breast, devouring every bit of moisture as if I were dying of thirst. I was lost in an insatiable need, and it seemed that the more I drank, the thirstier I became. I was moaning with both need and pleasure, and so could barely hear the sounds coming from Erica.

Finally her husky words broke through. "Here," she said, "drink from here."

I looked up to see that now her robe had fallen completely away, and my heart flipped over dangerously. She touched her thigh, letting her fingers trail languorously toward the point in question.

My throat constricted, the longing so deep and unbearable that I nearly choked with desire.

3RD DEGREE

A CASSIDY JAMES MYSTERY

by
KATE CALLOWAY

THE NAIAD PRESS, INC.
1997

Printed in the United States of America on acid-free paper
First Edition

Editor: Christine Cassidy
Cover designer: Bonnie Liss (Phoenix Graphics)
Typesetter: Sandi Stancil

Library of Congress Cataloging-in-Publication Data

Calloway, Kate. 1957 –
    Third Degree : a Cassidy James mystery \ by Kate Calloway.
        p.   cm.
    ISBN 1-56280-185-6 (pbk.)
    I. Title.
PS3553.A4245T48   1997
813′.54—dc21   97-10811
                                                                               CIP

For my family,
both immediate and extended

Acknowledgments

Thanks to the people who aided and abetted, offering advice, information and support. Every author relies on the honesty of good friends and I am lucky that so many of mine are willing and able to be a part of this. My co-conspirators include: Carol, Lyn, Linda, Carolyn, Murrell, Glenda, Deva and, of course, my editor, Christi. As always, my heart-felt thanks.

About the Author

Kate Calloway is the author of the Cassidy James Mystery Series, including *First Impressions* and *Second Fiddle*. She has also written short stories published by Naiad, and is a poet and song-writer in her spare time. Splitting her time between Southern California and the Pacific Northwest, she is a teacher, food-lover and wine enthusiast. The next installment in the Cassidy James series, *Fourth Down,* is due out soon.

Chapter One

I could hear their labored breathing behind me and knew they were gaining on me. I kicked the mustang, willing her forward toward the fence. If she could clear it before they caught up, I might have a chance. But I didn't trust her. She was a green two-year-old with a real penchant for bucking. Not only that, she was ornery and half-wild. Her only saving grace was that she flat-out loved to run.

I kicked her again and she laid her ears back menacingly. The fence was only twenty yards away and as I readied myself for the jump, her muscles bunched beneath the saddle. I could hear Sheriff Booker swearing at his horse to catch up. For one brief, exhilarating moment, I felt the beginning of what was about to be a perfect jump. And then the muscles somehow unbunched themselves at the last second and I went hurtling through the air, over the fence without the horse.

I hit the ground hard and rolled, instinctively sheltering my head from the thundering hooves of Booker's horse as he came gliding over the fence behind me. He missed me by about a foot.

"You okay?" Booker asked, reining his Appaloosa to a halt and circling back to where I lay sprawled on the ground. I noticed his mustache was twitching and he was having a hard time keeping a straight face.

"Just fine, thanks." I pushed myself off the ground and winced. Nothing appeared to be broken but I was quite sure my backside was already turning an interesting shade of bluish green.

"For a second there, I thought she was gonna do it," Booker said, losing the battle with the grin that had been struggling to break through. "I told you that little filly was a handful."

I walked back to the fence and unlatched the gate, letting myself through to the other side. The mustang stood innocently munching a mouthful of grass, her devilish eyes watching me with studied nonchalance. I was tempted to whack her a good one.

I led her through the gate and pulled myself into the saddle, already feeling the bruises. I reached down and patted her neck, ignoring Booker, who had finally succumbed to full-fledged laughter. His horse

2

was still panting heavily, while the mustang had barely broken a sweat.

"I know who's gonna need to soak in the hot tub tonight," he said, laughing. "I can taste them ice cold brewskies right now." It looked like I owed him a case of Weinhard's Special Reserve.

On the other hand, no one had said anything about having to go over the fence, I thought. He'd gone over, and I'd gone through. Well, actually, I'd gone over too. It was my horse that had decided she'd rather use the gate. But there was still a good half-mile left to the end of the race, and just because he was sitting there thinking he'd already won didn't mean I had to agree. I reached back and rubbed my neck, groaning.

"You sure you're okay?" he said, bringing the Appaloosa up beside me. His grin had vanished. Even better, he was facing back toward the fence, away from the finish line.

"Hey! Look at that!" I pointed toward the woods.

Booker turned and when he did, I kicked the mustang and let out the best Indian war cry I could muster. She responded beautifully, and the two of us flew past him, leaving Sheriff Booker literally in our dust.

To the wild whoops and hollers of our friends, I crossed the finish line a good five lengths in front of him. Booker was alternately cursing and laughing as he crossed.

"Cassidy James, you are one lousy cheat!" he said, patting his poor horse's sweaty neck. Booker was almost as winded as his horse. He'd been shouting and cursing at me the whole way back. I had trouble catching my own breath, I was laughing so hard. The mustang was the only one who seemed unaffected by the race.

"Guess you're gonna owe Cass a case of beer, Sheriff," Jess Martin said, coming over to congratulate me. Like the rest of us, he was wearing Levi's and boots. His long brown hair was pulled back in a ponytail and his beard was at its usual two-day stubble.

Little Jessie came running up behind him, looking like a miniature version of her father, minus the beard. "I had my money on you all the way, Cass!" she shouted, jumping up on the fence. "Dr. Carradine owes me ten bucks!" She was only eleven, but her bank account was in better shape than her father's.

"You bet against me?" I said to Maggie Carradine. She was looking pretty sheepish, but damned attractive I thought. She had a teal blouse tucked into her jeans, and the color almost matched her eyes.

"I bet against that beast you were riding!" she said. I'd made Maggie ride the horse once, and she'd been bucked off almost immediately.

"I suppose you bet against me, too?" I said, looking at Booker's wife, Rosie.

She was a distinguished-looking woman, with a mixture of Spanish and Aztec blood that gave her the bronze skin and fierce flashing eyes of her ancestors. She smiled apologetically. "Only one dollar," she said. "I never bet against Tom."

Booker slid off the Appaloosa and put his arm around his wife. In their fifties, they were a striking couple. His flowing silver hair and dazzling blue eyes were a sharp contrast to her dark Latin features.

Booker led the way back to the patio, telling

4

everyone how I'd tricked him, and going into great, exaggerated detail about my being flung like a sack of potatoes over the fence. By the time we gathered around the table, everyone was laughing.

Rosie brought out a couple of platters of her indecently delicious Muenster-stuffed poblano chiles, and for the next half-hour the good-natured banter was accompanied by assorted moans of pleasure. This was only the first of what would be a long succession of Mexican delicacies and I tried to pace myself, knowing I'd be sorry if I was too stuffed to eat the tamales and *carne asada* later.

"Come on," I said to Maggie, finally pushing myself away from the table. "Let's go for a walk. Maybe we can work off a few calories to make room for Rosie's tamales." We excused ourselves from the others and made our way toward the lake.

Booker's ranch lay on the outskirts of Cedar Hills and was accessible by both boat and car. His front yard looked out onto a lush valley surrounded by tall cedar and Douglas fir. His back yard was on one of the last and most secluded arms of Rainbow Lake. I lived about a mile away, in another cove. Since I had no road access, I'd brought Maggie by boat.

Maggie and I were in an awkward state, somewhere between lovers and friends. Everyone I knew was trying to help us back into the lover-state, including Booker and Rosie, who kept inviting the two of us over, but Maggie was resisting. The problem wasn't us, though. It was Erica Trinidad.

From the moment we'd met, Maggie and I had hit it off. She was everything I wanted in a woman — smart, sexy, fun and good-hearted. To top it off, she had her head on straight, which normally would have been a big plus. But it was her very "togetherness" that was keeping us apart. Because no matter how hard I tried to convince her otherwise, Maggie worried that I was still in love with Erica Trinidad.

"I know what I want," I'd told her more than once. "I want you."

"Sure you do," she'd answered in that calm, wise shrink-voice that drove me crazy. "But you also want Erica Trinidad. It's in your eyes, Cass. I see it, even if you don't."

"Bullshit!" I tend to resort to profanity when flustered.

"I told you before," she'd gone on serenely, "I'm not into martyrdom, but I'm also not into sadomasochism. I just want you to be sure. When you decide you really want me, I don't want you changing your mind."

One of the drawbacks of dating a psychologist is that they tend to act like they know more about you than you know yourself. It's also very difficult to actually win an argument. Even after you've made a seemingly brilliant point, they just nod and smile, like they've been waiting for you to get around to saying whatever it was you just said.

What saved Maggie from being unbearable, though, was that she was genuinely good inside. And she directed her laser beam insights as much at herself as she did at me.

As we walked down the pebbled path toward the lake and horse corrals, I slipped my arm around her waist. We were about the same height, but Maggie was full of soft curves, while I tended toward the lean and muscled look. Not that she wasn't athletic. Maggie was a true adventure-loving thrill-seeker. She liked to climb mountains, jump from airplanes and scuba dive. Last month she'd tried to talk me into bungee jumping. It had been a very short conversation. Now, as we walked along, drinking in the beautiful Oregon scenery, she leaned into my arm.

"How big is this place, anyway?"

"It must be over twenty acres," I said. "But in the winter, about a third of it is under water. That's why they built their house on stilts. Last winter, I drove my boat right up to their front porch."

I led her around to the last corral where a big red mare had her nose buried in hay, while a spindly-legged colt nursed contentedly. In the next stall I noticed that the mustang, true to form, had rolled in the mud right after Marcos, the ranch hand, had finished grooming her. When she saw me, she gave a belligerent snort and then reared up and whinnied. Either she was awfully glad to see me, or she was letting me know how she felt about jumping fences. Maggie laughed out loud at the antics.

"Don't encourage her," I said. I looked around to make sure Marcos was nowhere in sight. Except for the rebellious mustang, it seemed we were all alone. I pulled Maggie toward me, letting my fingers trail through her dark curly hair. She came into my arms after a brief hesitation, and we kissed with passion.

Suddenly there was a noise behind us, and we pulled apart in time to see little Jessie running hard down the path.

"Damn," Maggie murmured.

"Cassidy! Come quick!" Jessie was short of breath. "Rosie says someone's on the phone for you and they sound scared."

I looked at Maggie and shrugged. I wasn't even sure who knew I was here. My best friend Martha had been invited, but ever since being promoted to detective on the Kings Harbor Police Force, she'd been putting in longer hours, trying to prove they'd made the right decision. Just about everyone else I really cared about was right here, except, of course, Erica Trinidad. And I seriously doubted the call would be from her.

Erica was still in town, living at her uncle's place out on the lake, not five minutes away from my own house, but she'd been steering clear of me all summer. In fact, I'd only seen her twice since the day she'd come waltzing back into Cedar Hills, apparently assuming that I'd be waiting for her like a loyal dog. When I'd told her I was involved with someone else, she seemed genuinely crushed.

Not that I was about to feel sorry for her. She'd been gallivanting around Southern California with some famous woman movie director for nine months while I'd waited for her to return. The problem was, patience never has been one of my virtues.

"Come on! Rosie says it sounds like an emergency!"

Maggie and I ran behind her and when we got to the house, Rosie was inside the kitchen, pacing.

"She hung up," Rosie said when we entered. "Wouldn't even leave her name. Said she'd call back in ten minutes. But, Cass, it sounded like someone I know. I just can't place the voice. Whoever it is has been crying."

8

"Not Martha," I said, worried.

"Oh, no. I'd know her voice. And besides, she'd have told me who it was."

A few minutes later the phone rang, and I snatched it off the wall. "This is Cassidy James."

"Cassie. Thank God. I need to see you right away." The voice was strained, filled with something between anger and fear. And even though I'd never seen or heard her so upset before, I recognized Lizzie Thompson's voice immediately.

"Where are you?" I asked, turning away from Maggie and Rosie, who were looking at me with raised brows.

"I'm at home. Please don't say anything to anyone, Cass. I know everyone is over there. This is personal. Please, just make some excuse to get away and come over here." Before I could answer, the phone went dead. Lizzie wasn't giving me the opportunity to say no.

"Well?" Rosie said, hands on her hips, her dark eyes full of concern.

"It's a client," I said. "Unfortunately, she asked me to keep this confidential. I'm afraid I'm going to have to go."

"Is everything okay?" Maggie asked, following me to the door.

"I don't know. I'll try to call you as soon as I can. If I'm not back by the time you're ready to leave, can you get a ride with Jess?"

"Don't give it another thought," she said.

I started jogging toward the boat dock, and Maggie kept up with me.

"This isn't one of those things that requires a gun, is it?" she asked.

9

"I don't know anything yet," I said. The last case I'd been on, I'd nearly gotten us both killed. I could understand why Maggie might be a little nervous.

"Just one more question, Cass."

I hopped into my blue open-bow Sea Swirl while she untied the bow line.

"This doesn't have anything to do with Erica Trinidad, does it?"

I looked into her lovely green eyes, and smiled reassuringly. "It definitely does not."

But as I pulled away from the dock, I couldn't ignore the fact that my heart had pounded at the thought that the call might be from Erica.

Chapter Two

It was almost five o' clock by the time I pulled up to the county dock, and because it was Sunday, most of the weekenders had already headed back for the city. There were still quite a few locals fishing from the pier, and a handful of families had spread blankets on the park lawn. People lazed in the late afternoon sun and I could smell hamburgers sizzling on the barbecues nearby. It was late August and people were trying to squeeze every ounce out of what remained of summer.

I'd never been to Lizzie Thompson's house, but I

knew where she lived. It was my habit to walk the streets of Cedar Hills as often as possible, and I recognized almost everyone's house because of it. Lizzie spent most of her time at Logger's Tavern, which she owned and ran. For a bartender, who was both popular and outgoing on the job, she seemed an intensely private woman — one of those people adept at listening to other people's life stories without revealing much about their own. I often suspected that she'd have been better off running a woman's bar, but this was pure speculation on my part. She was in her forties, which should have been old enough to know what she wanted. She knew I was gay, as did quite a few other people in town, and every now and then, I thought she might actually be coming on to me, but I did my best to discourage anything more than a friendship with her. At the moment, I had all the women in my life I could handle.

I turned down Main Street and headed for Osprey Lane. From there, it was only a few blocks to Third Street, and Lizzie's house was about half-way down on the left. When I knocked on the door, I noticed a movement behind the living room curtains and a moment later the door opened a crack.

She didn't say a word, just motioned me in and locked the door behind me. I'd never seen such a change in a person in my life. Normally confident and energetic, Lizzie walked with the shuffled gait of someone who'd been given too much Thorazine. But it was her eyes that had me most alarmed. They were wild and full of fear.

"Lizzie, what happened?" I asked, following her into the kitchen.

She sat in a wooden chair, put her head in her hands and proceeded to sob. I wasn't sure what to do. I put my hand on her shoulder and left it there. Finally, her sobs subsided and I pulled up a chair across from her.

"Thanks for coming," she said, wiping her face on her sleeve. She blew her nose in an already sopping wet paper towel and tried to smile. It nearly broke my heart.

"Please, Lizzie. You've got to tell me what happened."

"I need you to find someone," she finally said, looking directly at me. Her eyes had a crazed determination, and I wondered if she'd gone completely around the bend.

"Find someone?"

"I want to hire you to find the one who, who . . ." Her mouth twisted with rage as she tried to find a way to say it.

"Who what?" I asked as gently as possible.

"I'm not sure what to call it!" She was on the verge of hysteria. Her eyes were red-rimmed and glassy and I could almost smell her fear.

"I don't know how to explain what happened," she said more quietly, sounding defeated. "I'm not even sure what did happen."

Again, she started to weep, and I was at a loss for words. Lizzie was normally so strong and stoic. I couldn't imagine what could bring her to such despair.

"Were you hurt?" I finally asked.

Her eyes shot up at me with wild fury. It was as if I'd asked a question for which there was no correct answer. Finally, with a great deal of coaxing, I got her to tell me what had happened.

Lizzie had returned from grocery shopping at about two o'clock. She was bringing the last two sacks into the kitchen when she heard a noise behind her. Startled, she turned in time to see the flash of some kind of rod, wielded by a man wearing a ski mask. She dropped the sacks and prepared to fight off her attacker.

Lizzie was a strong woman, unafraid of physical confrontation. But her first swing was met with the devastating shock of an electrical jolt that surged through her body and dropped her to the floor in a crumpled heap. The next thing she remembered, she was lying face down on her bedroom floor, spread-eagle and completely naked. Her hands and feet had been tied to the bed frame and dresser, and there was some kind of rag stuffed into her mouth.

"I didn't realize until later," she said, her strong chin quivering, "that he'd used my own underwear to gag me."

The hair on the back of my neck was standing at attention, and my insides were churning.

"He used nylons to tie my wrists and ankles, so I couldn't move. I think what scared me the most was that he didn't blindfold me. In all those movies, it's the ones that don't blindfold their victims that intend to kill them."

"Go on," I encouraged, trying not to appear impatient.

"I think he wanted me to see him," she continued. "I mean, he had his head covered with the ski mask, so I couldn't see his face, but he kept parading back and forth in front of me, like he was showing off."

"What did he do?" I blurted. I couldn't help myself. This was driving me crazy.

"Nothing!" she wailed. "At least not to me. But he went through my closet and took out one of my belts. Then he started beating my pillow. Really laid into it. I kept waiting for him to hit me, but he never did." It took a few minutes for her to calm down enough to continue. "Cassidy, I'm telling you. I thought I was a dead woman. I thought he would rape me and then kill me. Why else would I be naked, but allowed to see? I kept tugging at the nylons, trying to pull free. I have a loaded thirty-eight under the bed."

I nodded, beginning to comprehend the intensity of the fear she must have experienced. From her eyes, I knew the fear wasn't gone just because the man was.

"After he finally quit whipping the pillow, I could hear him humming. At first, I couldn't figure it out, but that's what he was doing. Like he was happy. Real relaxed. As if he belonged in my house."

"What was he doing?" I asked again, more softly.

"I don't know!" Her voice was finally breaking. "I think he was making himself at home!"

"What?" I was having a lot of trouble with this.

"He turned on music. He took a bath. He fixed himself a sandwich from the groceries I'd just bought. He lay down on my bed and ate the sandwich. He even had chips. I could see him. I could hear him. I could even smell him. I just couldn't get up and kill him!"

"Did he hurt you in any way?" My stomach had ceased to churn. It was now a solid mass of steel. Like I'd swallowed a bowling ball.

Lizzie shook her head, tears streaming silently down her cheeks. "I managed to get one arm almost free, but I couldn't reach my gun. Even so, I was ready for him. If he came after me, I'd have killed him. Or died trying. But he didn't seem interested in me that way. It was like he was acting out some weird play, and I was his audience."

A captive audience, no less, I thought, but spared Lizzie this obvious insight. She was finally letting the tears fall freely, and I reached out and held her hand while she cried. It wasn't nearly enough, but it was all that I could think to do. When she finally pulled away, I got up and went to her liquor cabinet, hoping to find something strong and mellow. For a bartender, she had a pretty pathetic selection. I finally settled for some ancient-looking cherry brandy. Stifling a grimace, I poured us each a half-snifter and watched as Lizzie gulped hers gratefully.

"I'll need to ask you some questions."

She nodded, wiping at her tears as if she were suddenly embarrassed to be caught showing emotion.

"Do you have any idea who it was?"

She shook her head. "The ski mask covered his whole head. Even his eyes were covered, except for the pupils. I can't even say what color his eyes were. And he had on those white, latex-type gloves. I think he knows me, though."

"Why is that?" I was taking hurried notes on a pad I'd found by the phone.

"The tune he was humming. Cass, it's so scary. He was humming my favorite song. That one by Billy Ray Cyrus about an achy breaky heart. Everyone knows I love that stupid thing. They get a big kick out of it. Always put it on the juke box and sing it to me. I think whoever was here has also been in the tavern. And I think he wanted me to know that he knows me."

I let the enormity of that sink in.

"I got the feeling that he felt like he owned me. Owned my house and everything in it. That he could do anything he wanted. And you know what?" She looked at me with huge eyes, still wild but infinitely sad. "He could have. He could have killed me three times over. And I wouldn't have been able to do a thing to stop him. He didn't have to hurt me, Cassidy. It was enough that he terrorized me."

It took nearly two hours to satisfy myself that I knew all Lizzie could tell me about her intruder. I knew he was probably over six feet and fairly big. I knew he wore some kind of cologne, but that it didn't quite mask the body odor beneath it. Maybe that's why he had bathed, I thought. I knew he wore light gray sweats and tennis shoes. I knew he had worn a pair of latex gloves, presumably to avoid leaving fingerprints. And I knew, after really pushing Lizzie about this, that he had not only ransacked the house, but that he'd taken something with him.

"It's too embarrassing," she'd said, for the third time. "He knew it, too. That's why he took it."

"Took what? For God's sake, Lizzie."

17

She spoke the word so softly, I hardly heard her. But I didn't make her repeat it. The intruder had found Lizzie's vibrator.

I started to smile until I saw the look of sheer anguish on her face. She must have thought she was the only woman in Cedar Hills who owned one. And evidently she was mortified that I now knew about it. I was about to allay her fears when she went on.

"He turned it on. That's how I knew he'd found it," she said, blushing. "Before he left, he came up to me and held it to his lips, going 'shshshsh.' Up until then, he hadn't said a word. The way he did it, I knew he was threatening me. Don't ask me how I knew, I just did. He was saying, if you tell anyone, I'll be back. Then he just disappeared, leaving me tied up where I was. It took me another half-hour to get myself free."

It was nearly dark when Lizzie excused herself, saying what she really needed was a hot shower. I asked her not to use the bathroom the intruder had used, and she looked relieved. She had refused my suggestion that we go to the police, and I knew it was pointless to pursue the matter, even though they'd be better equipped to handle evidence than I was. Well, I'd just have to do the best I could with what I had. I helped myself to a handful of Baggies and headed for the bathroom.

If the man had bathed, I knew there was a good chance he'd left some hair in the tub. Unfortunately, the first thing I noticed was the can of Comet and the wet sponge sitting on the sink counter. He'd scrubbed the entire bathroom thoroughly. Was this guy a neat-freak, I wondered, or was he just very careful not to leave any evidence behind?

I used the screwdriver on my Swiss Army knife to pry up the bathtub drain and carefully emptied the gooey wad of hair and scum into one of the Baggies. I had no intention of humiliating Lizzie by going through the yucky mess in front of her. I pocketed the Baggie and replaced the drain.

If there'd ever been a wet footprint on the bathmat, it had long since dried. There were no visible fingerprints on the chrome surfaces, no physical evidence anywhere that I could see. Still, why had he taken such a risk, using the bathtub at all? Had he bathed with his mask and gloves on? Why the need to bathe in the first place? She'd said he had a peculiar body odor. Had he used her soap? The more questions I asked myself, the crazier the whole thing seemed. Still, I felt sure that the fact he'd taken a bath, and had been so careful to leave no clues, were somehow clues in themselves.

I went through the rest of the house, room by room, hoping against hope that the man had left behind something tangible. I could tell he'd handled some of Lizzie's knickknacks because the dust pattern on the shelves didn't match the exact spots where he'd replaced them. But with the latex gloves, this wasn't any help at all.

I gathered up the nylons he'd used on her hands and feet. They looked like your standard, tan-colored pantyhose, probably large enough to be queen size. I bagged them and continued my search.

I checked the area immediately outside the back door and even in the dark it didn't take me long to find where he'd hidden while waiting for Lizzie to get home. Just to the left of the back porch was a four-foot hedge of thistleberry running the entire length of the house. It was tall enough to conceal someone hiding on the two-foot-wide strip of dirt between the house and the hedge.

The dirt was blessedly damp, a perfect surface for footprints. Unfortunately, the intruder had obliterated his prints by deliberately scuffling them before he left. This man was not only smart, I decided, he was thorough. It was on the bottom step leading to the carport that I discovered something else about the intruder. A small rust-throated robin lay lifeless on the concrete, its tiny neck snapped in two. A parting gift? A threat? Either way, it sent goosebumps right through me.

Lizzie was in the bathroom a long time, long enough for me to pick up the mess in the bedroom and finish putting away the groceries. I continued to look for clues as I went, but I wasn't holding my breath. Even so, I took careful inventory as I worked.

I'd always been curious about Lizzie, and her house surprised me. For such a tough woman, she had surprisingly feminine tastes. Her curtains were lacy and her bedspread was a sea of pink flowers. There was an old teddy bear propped between the two pillows, with half an ear missing. It looked as though it had gotten her through many a lonely night. Her artwork was primarily inexpensive, store-bought stuff, and when I checked out her music collection, I found mostly country western cassettes. Next to her bed, I found a dog-eared romance novel she had almost finished.

Suddenly, I felt guilty for this invasion of her privacy, and I went to wait in the kitchen. I was shaken by what had happened to her and somehow it seemed even worse, now that I'd discovered that beneath the tough exterior, Lizzie was a soft-hearted romantic.

I sat down at the table and stared at my notes, trying to make some sense of the whole thing. I knew I should be concentrating on who, but all I could think about was why. Why would someone break into someone else's house, terrorize her, lie in her bed, sit in her tub, eat her food, listen to her music, hum her favorite song, steal her vibrator, and after beating her pillow with a belt, leave a dead bird on her step? I thought I understood a thing or two about the criminal mind, but this seemed something far worse. I was in over my head, and I knew it.

But the idea that there was some sicko-psycho running loose in Cedar Hills did more than chill me to the bone. It made me mad. This was my town. Lizzie was my friend. I found myself clenching my fists.

I poured myself another shot of the cherry brandy and it occurred to me that it was actually starting to taste pretty good.

When she came out, Lizzie looked thoroughly scrubbed and exhausted. She had dressed herself in men's pajamas, which seemed a strange contrast to all the frilly decorations but suited her to a tee. She wore slippers with little dog faces on them that made me smile.

"Don't laugh," she said. "They were a gift from my mother." But to my relief she was laughing herself, and I hoped the worst was over.

"I can make up a bed on the couch," I offered.

She looked at me crossly. "What? And move in

tomorrow?" There was sarcasm in her voice. "I'm not an invalid, Cass. And I've been living alone for a long time. I've got a Colt forty-five down at the bar and a thirty-eight under my bed. Believe me, the bastard won't get a second chance. I'm not afraid of him. In fact, I'd welcome his return."

"Revenge can't undo what he did," I said gently. But I remembered how I had felt the time a couple of Nazi-worshipping teenagers had kidnapped my cats, and I understood the fury that could drive someone to seek revenge. I decided not to mention the dead bird for the moment. She had enough on her mind.

Lizzie smiled sadly, tugging at her damp hair. "Right now, I just want to get some sleep," she said. "I can't thank you enough for coming over. I really do feel much better. I know there's probably nothing you can do to find out who did this. When I called, I wasn't thinking straight."

"Well, I'd like to try, anyway," I said, surprising myself. The truth was, I doubted I could do any good at all. I wanted more than anything to talk with Maggie. She had a way of seeing things that helped me put them in perspective. I fussed around some more, making sure all her doors and windows were locked, and even heated up a can of chicken noodle soup before she finally kicked me out.

"Call me if you need anything at all," I said.

"I will, Cassidy. Now go on home."

I'm not normally the mothering type, but she just looked so damned vulnerable with those silly puppy dog slippers on, I couldn't help myself. I leaned down and kissed her on the forehead. I shouldn't have done it, though, because I could have sworn I heard her start crying again as I let myself out into the cool, dark night.

I hurried all the way back to the county dock, shivering not so much from the cold as from the creepy feeling that something sinister was lurking in the darkness of Cedar Hills.

Chapter Three

I awoke to the sonorous purring of Gammon, my portly cat, who lay sprawled on my stomach, her claws rhythmically piercing my skin through the thin sheets. This was her way of saying it was breakfast time. Panic, her sleek, athletic sister, was perched on my pillow, biting my hair. The wake-up crew was in full swing.

I pulled on a pair of old blue sweats and headed for the bathroom where both cats leaped up onto the counter, eager to help me get organized for the day.

They were a striking pair, half-Bengal and half-Egyptian Mau. They'd been bred for their spots, but it was their coloring that made them so unusual. Gammon was a rich caramel bronze with brown spots and silver ticking. Panic had silver ticking too, but her spots were nearly black, and her tail was exceptionally long. They looked like something straight out of the jungle, but while Panic indeed had a wild streak, Gammon was as docile as a big old dog. Between them, they kept me laughing, even through the worst of times.

As I went through my usual morning routine, I studied my reflection. My thirty-second birthday was coming up, and I'd begun to notice a few gray hairs at my temples to go with the laugh lines around my eyes. Other than that, I was looking pretty fit, I thought. My blond hair was nearly as light as when I was a kid, thanks to all the time I spent in the sun. And physically, I'd never been in better shape. Except for the bruises on my rear end from yesterday's fall, I didn't look too bad.

Besides my daily trek through Cedar Hills, I rode a stationary bike most nights, practiced rudimentary martial arts at least three times a week, and in general liked to work and play hard. It was a good thing, because I was also an avid cook and liked nothing more than to gorge on good food. My best friend, Martha, who had always battled her weight, was forever furious at me for my lucky metabolism, especially since she loved to eat as much as I did. We were a bit like Gammon and Panic, I thought. Why one cat had turned out skinny and the other hadn't was just another of life's little mysteries.

I gave myself one last, cursory glance in the mirror, deciding that "cute" was as good as I was ever going to get, and headed for the kitchen.

Outside, the day was already warm and sunny. After feeding the cats, I let them outside and went about fixing my own breakfast. Having missed out on Rosie's main courses last night, I was fairly famished. I rummaged around in the refrigerator until I found what I wanted.

I diced a brown onion and let it saute in olive oil before tossing in a handful of chopped red bell pepper, some sliced mushrooms and a few chunks of my own home-grown tomato. I whipped an egg until it was frothy and added it to the pan, tossing in a little crumbled goat cheese for good measure. By now, the cats were back, rubbing against my ankles like crazy. It was their way of telling me that they preferred my version of breakfast to their own.

When the omelette was golden-brown, I poured myself a glass of orange juice and went out on the front deck to enjoy my breakfast in the sun while the cats entertained me with their frolicking antics on the lawn. I tried to let my mind free-float, hoping something brilliant would leap out at me. Unfortunately, the only leaping was done by Panic, who surprised me with a fat field mouse. This brought to mind the image of the dead robin on Lizzie's back step and sent me back into the house for a second cup of coffee and my notebook.

I made two lists; one for what I knew and one for what I wondered. The latter list was by far longer and after a while I gave up and did what I had really wanted to do all along. I called Maggie.

"How's the sexiest private investigator I know?" she asked when she heard my voice.

"You really think I'm sexy?" I asked hopefully. "I had just come to the conclusion that I was destined to be plain old cute the rest of my life."

She laughed, her voice husky. "Actually, you're that too. I'd say you're cute in a sexy kind of way."

Now you know why I was crazy about Maggie Carradine. We fooled around like that for a while, and then I told her about the case. I didn't mention Lizzie's name, but beyond that, I told her almost everything. She listened patiently, and when I finished, I heard her let out a huge sigh. When the silence lasted more than a few seconds, I couldn't stand it.

"Well?" I demanded. "What do you think?"

"I think I have a real moral dilemma here."

"What do you mean?"

"I mean, I've heard a similar story before. Twice, in fact. Because of client confidentiality, I can't really say any more."

"No way. Are you saying that one of your clients had this same experience?" I asked. My voice had risen at least a decibel.

"Cass, this is very touchy territory. I'm bound by law to protect my client's confidentiality. You of all people should know that."

"I do, Maggie. But this is incredible. There's got to be a way for you to tell me what you know without revealing their identities. After all, I'm supposed to protect my client's confidentiality too. Which is why I didn't tell you who called me last night. That doesn't mean I can't share parts of the case with you." I knew I was sounding defensive, but I couldn't help it. Maggie was about to pull a holier-than-me routine. It was like playing strip poker with someone who, after watching you strip to your skivvies, decides they're tired of the game.

I heard her take in another deep breath, letting it out slowly. I waited.

"Don't ask me one single question, because I'm not going to get tricked into saying more than I'm about to tell you. Understood?"

"Understood," I said, my heart pounding.

"Okay. First off, I've heard this same story twice, from two different people. The first time was nearly two years ago. The woman who came to see me was very agitated. She hadn't slept in weeks. When I suggested she go to the police, she refused but wouldn't tell me why. I only saw her that one time and never heard from her again. Her story was very similar to the one you just told me, although it sounds like he wasn't quite as bold two years ago. Perhaps he's gained confidence with time. Oh, and there were a couple of other differences. As far as I know, he didn't leave any dead animal behind, although maybe she just didn't mention that part. Also, the man took something with him when he left."

I hadn't told Maggie about the vibrator, but now I did.

"I can't tell you what he took from her, Cass, so don't ask, okay? I'm hesitant to admit this, but at the time, I thought it was possible that the woman was delusional or maybe just an attention seeker. When she didn't come back, I thought that was probably the case. Then, just last month, a second woman came to see me with nearly the same story. I can tell you, I felt terrible for having doubted the first woman's sincerity. I'm still working with the second woman, and I really can't tell you any more about it except, like the first woman, this one refuses to go to the police. I hope this helps you."

"Did he take something from the second woman too?" I asked.

"Cass."

"Well, at least tell me whether there was a dead animal, Maggie. This is important."

Silence. Then another long sigh.

"Okay, okay," I said. "I understand you can't answer that. Jesus, Maggie. Do you realize what this means? If it's the same guy, and I'd bet any amount of money that it is, then he's been doing this for two years or longer! Why hasn't anyone gone to the police?"

"Are you sure they haven't?" It was a good question. Lizzie hadn't gone, and neither had Maggie's two clients, but that didn't mean others hadn't. And there had to be others, I felt certain.

"Why, Maggie?" I asked. "What would make someone want to do something like this? It just doesn't make any sense to me."

"You can't try to make sense out of something irrational. Obviously we're dealing with a very troubled mind. What seems illogical to us may seem perfectly rational to him. Something in his own life experience, perhaps, has created this need to . . . to intrude upon people in their homes and to have power over them. It's impossible to know. Even he may not know why he's doing it. But one thing I think is safe to assume. If he has been doing this for the last two years, he probably can't stop himself. Most likely, he'll escalate his activities until he's caught. I just hope he's caught before he escalates them too far. Already I see a progression, based on what you've told me compared to my two cases. He's definitely getting bolder, which could be dangerous for his next victim. The anger he's acting out, by whipping the bed, could end up being taken out on the victim instead."

Not to mention the dead bird, I thought. In her own way, Maggie had just let me know that her current client had not been the recipient of a dead animal.

Using every ounce of charm I could muster, I tried to convince Maggie to let me question her client, even if only over the phone anonymously. Her answer was swift and vehement. Finally, after much backpedaling, I got her to agree to at least inform her present client of my investigation. I hung up feeling both frustrated and stymied. How was I supposed to find this guy if no one would talk to me!

I couldn't even canvass the damn neighborhood to find out if anyone had seen anything unusual. When I'd told Lizzie the night before that that's what I intended to do, she'd come unglued.

"You can't, Cassidy. Someone will link your questions to me. And as soon as they do, the whole town will know I hired you. How long do you think it will be before the rumors start flying? I don't want anyone to know this happened, period. I don't want to go to work every day of my life wondering which of my customers is thinking about me lying naked on my floor while some creep revs up my vibrator." Her cheeks had turned a violent shade of crimson.

I tried to convince her she that had nothing to be ashamed of but Lizzie just glared at me until I gave up. Shamed was exactly how she felt. Unfortunately, this limited my options.

Now, in the midst of my frustration, the inkling of an idea began to formulate. Before I did another thing, I needed to talk to both Martha and Booker. Besides being a police detective in Kings Harbor just ten miles away, Martha was my best friend in the whole world, so I decided to check with her first.

"Who was this?" she asked after I'd told her everything I could about last night's incident without mentioning Lizzie.

"You know I can't tell you that, Martha. Anyway, there's more." There was no way I could tell her that Maggie had even slightly violated a client's confidentiality, so I fudged it. "I have reason to believe that this guy has been doing this for some time. At least two years. Maybe you've run across something like this?"

Martha sighed. "Not as far as I know. But that doesn't mean someone else hasn't heard about it. Let me do some checking. I'll get back to you. Oh, and not to change the subject, but are you making any headway with my favorite ex-therapist?"

Sometimes I thought Martha was as in love with Maggie as I was.

"I'm still working on it," I said truthfully.

"Well, don't give up," she said, chuckling. "Sooner or later, you're bound to win her over." She hung up, leaving me holding a dead receiver.

I was about to call Booker when my phone rang. It was Lizzie.

"Listen," she said, "forget about last night, okay? It's better if we just let sleeping dogs lie."

"Lizzie, what if I told you you're not the only one he's done this to?"

"What?" I was sure she'd heard me.

"I mean, what if, since last night, I'd heard of at least two other identical cases. Wouldn't it stand to reason that there might be even more?"

"Cassidy James, if you told someone about this, I'll kill you. I swear I will."

"Now hold on, Lizzie. I didn't say I told anyone. I promised you confidentiality and that's what you'll get. But I am a private investigator. I do know how to find things out, okay? Give me some credit here."

This wasn't really lying, I told myself. Mild fibbing, perhaps, but for a good cause.

"Okay," she said. "I'm sorry I bit your head off. Are you saying he's done this same thing before? To other women?"

"I think he probably has, yes. Like you, they probably haven't told the police."

"But why?" she wailed.

I wasn't sure if she meant why had he done it, or why hadn't the women come forward. I took a chance. "He's sick," I said. "And he's smart. He knows, somehow, that they can't afford to tell the police. Like you, they're afraid."

"I never fucking said I was afraid!"

"No, you didn't. But you also didn't go to the

police. Listen, Lizzie. You're one of the strongest women I know. If this bastard can mess with your head so much that you won't go to the police, imagine what other women would do. In fact, I'd bet good money that there's even a few women right here in Cedar Hills who are being eaten alive with fear because this sicko came into their home, abused them psychologically and then left them afraid for their lives." I let that sink in, wondering if I really was on the right track.

Lizzie's response floored me. "You mean, it wasn't just me?" Her voice sounded tiny, like a six-year-old's. It was as if this were the only part of what I'd said that she had finally managed to process.

"I don't think so, no."

"But how can you be sure?"

"Well, I'm doing a check right now to see if any-one has reported something like this to the police in Kings Harbor, and I need to check with Sheriff Booker, too."

"Cass, I told you. No police. I don't want Booker to know. He's a friend!"

"I'd never mention your name, Lizzie. You know that. But to catch this guy, I've got to talk to some-one else who's been through this, and right now, I don't know who they are. Without other witnesses, I just don't have enough to go on. Besides," I added, starting to smile, "I'd like to shake this guy up a little. Make him crawl out of his hidey hole."

"What do you mean?"

"I mean, if I'm right, this guy is not only smart, he's cocky. He's been getting away with tormenting women a long time. And he thinks he can get away with it forever. No one has challenged him. I want to trip him up a little, make him sweat. Sometimes people do funny things, start making mistakes, when they're out of their comfort zone."

"How? How would you do this?" She sounded petrified.

I swallowed hard, knowing that what I was about to tell her sounded crazy. "I want to put out a flier asking other victims to come forward." This was met with utter silence, so I went on.

"Lizzie, listen. You're not the only one. You didn't go to the police. My guess is that there are others who also didn't go. I want to talk to them. It's that simple. Without help, I'll just have to wait until he does it again to someone else. Even then, there's no guarantee that person will come forward. I need to ask for their help."

"You think someone would come forward? If you asked?"

"Police can't necessarily guarantee confidentiality, but I can. People can talk to me anonymously if they want. The thing is, I know there are women out there who can help us, but I don't know who they are. I need their help. And if I'm right, I think they might need mine."

To my surprise, she started to laugh.

"What?" I asked. "What's so funny?"

"It just might work at that," she said. "But it's kind of ironic, don't you think?"

"How so?"

"Well, you're proposing a sort of blackmail," she said. I wasn't sure I wanted to hear this. "You expect women who have already been victimized to come forward out of guilt, by saying that if they don't, it will be their fault if someone else gets victimized like

34

they did. I like you, Cass, but sometimes I think you drive an awfully hard bargain."

I mulled this over, knowing in my heart she was right. It *was* a sort of emotional blackmail. But what other choice did I have? And besides, if it had been me, I'd want to know that I was not alone. Wouldn't I? The truth was, there was no way I could begin to know how I would feel. It hadn't happened to me.

"What do you think, Lizzie? I won't do this unless you feel okay with it."

"I don't know, Cass. On a selfish level, I'm afraid someone will connect your flier with what happened to me. That's something I just couldn't stand."

"But no one even knows I went to see you," I argued. "Rosie didn't recognize your voice, and I didn't tell anyone where I was going. Unless you tell someone, what happened last night will remain entirely between the two of us."

There was a long silence, which I refused to break. It was her decision. I'd done all the arm-twisting I was going to. Finally, when she did speak, her voice was low and determined.

"Okay, then," she said. "Let's get busy on those fliers. The sooner the better, as far as I'm concerned. I just want to put this whole damned thing behind me."

I could have hugged her. It took a strong woman to put her own fears aside, and Lizzie Thompson was proving herself to be just that. I only hoped that if there were others out there who had been intruded on by this man, then they too could find the strength to call me. I didn't know which was harder for me to believe — that Maggie's two clients and Lizzie could be the only victims, or that there *were* others and they'd all managed to keep the crime a secret. Cedar Hills was turning into a regular Peyton Place.

I sat down at my computer, trying to get the flier just right. I wanted it to stand out. I needed it to be noticed, to get people's attention, but most of all, I admitted, I wanted it to get the intruder's attention. Even if no one came forward, it was possible the intruder might panic and make a mistake. A long shot, I knew, but a long shot was better than no shot at all.

Finally, I settled for the following:

HAS AN INTRUDER
VIOLATED YOUR HOME?

Cassidy James, Private Investigator, is looking for anyone who might have information about crimes here in Cedar Hills. If someone has invaded your home and terrorized you, and for personal reasons you did not disclose this, please call the number below. No names are necessary. **Complete confidentiality assured.** Don't let this happen to someone else! **Together we can and must stop him now!**

I put my number across the bottom of the flier and saved it on my hard drive before I could change my mind.

Chapter Four

I managed to coax Panic and Gammon inside and
left them curled up on the window ledge when I
went into town. Mondays were slow on the lake, even
in August. The sky was a deep, brilliant blue with
not a cloud in sight. Osprey dove for fish, and giant
blue herons cruised the shore, their ungainly wings
batting the air in a slow, labored dance. There wasn't
another boat on the water, and I felt, as I often did,
that I had truly found a piece of paradise in Cedar
Hills. But as much as I enjoyed the sun beating
down on my shoulders and the spray of the water on

my face, I couldn't help but think that this paradise was being sullied by something evil.

The Cedar Hills Marina sits at the junction of Rainbow Lake and Rainbow Creek which runs about a mile west to the Pacific Ocean. Docking at the marina can be tricky when the tide is going out, as it was that morning. But living on the lake with no road access makes a pretty adept boat handler out of anyone, and I'd been doing this for over four years now. I eyeballed the available slips and chose one on the west side. I made a wide turn and pulled the throttle back into neutral, letting the boat glide into the slip and bump gently against the dock with hardly a jolt. Not bad, I thought, remembering how difficult I'd found this when I'd first moved here. After that first summer, the hull of my blue boat had been streaked with white, sure sign of a boating novice.

I hopped out of the boat, secured the ropes to the cleats and carried my house-trash up the ramp to the dumpsters provided for marina customers. Tommy Greene was standing in the driveway, hosing off his cherry-red Mustang.

"Mornin', Cass," he said, averting the spray to avoid drenching me.

"Looks good, Tommy. If you get bored, mine's right over there." I pointed my chin toward a rather dusty black Jeep Cherokee.

He laughed and scrunched up his merry eyes, making him look even more like one of Santa's little helpers. I'd always thought of Tommy as elf-like. Not just because he was short, but his ears were a little pointy, as was his chin, and his eyes had a perpetual twinkle. When he smiled, the picture was complete. I tried not to look at his arms and legs which were still scarred with recent burn marks. These were the result of an explosion meant for my last client, and poor Tommy had inadvertently gotten in the way. The once-tanned skin was now a patchwork quilt of raw, pink hairless puffs. The wounds still looked painful, though they appeared to be improving every day. Tommy seemed oblivious to them, at any rate.

"Goin' for your morning walk?" he asked. "You're off to kind of a late start, aren't you?"

"Yeah," I said. "The morning kind of got away from me."

I left Tommy and headed for the county library. It was just off Main Street, a small white plaster rectangle tucked between the newspaper office and the Rainbow Realty. Mrs. Peters, a white-haired lady in her late seventies, greeted me when I entered.

"Cassidy James. What can I help you with today?" she said, tottering over toward me. She was wearing a wildly flowered Hawaiian print shift which didn't quite go with her white stockings and thick-soled hospital-style shoes. She had a white sweater on over the shift, which helped calm it down a bit. In fact, if it hadn't been for the shift, Mrs. Peters would have been lost in a sea of white. Even her dentures were pearly. Ever since she'd helped me break a code by showing me how to find degrees of latitude and longitude, Mrs. Peters had considered herself something of a sleuth. Whenever I came into the library, her eyes lit up like a kid's at Christmas.

"Well, I'm afraid this morning I just need to use your Xerox machine." I showed her the flier and her eyes widened.

"Oh, my. Oh, my goodness," she said, clucking her tongue. "Is there anything I can do?"

"Can I post one of the fliers on your door?"

I knew she'd be disappointed that I didn't have a more interesting mission for her. But she was eager to help in any way she could, and she took the flier right out of my hand, making the copies for me.

"Let me know if I can be of further assistance," she said, patting my hand with dry, floury fingers.

I thanked her and let myself out of the tiny library, twenty-five copies of the flier tucked under my arm. I was about to head for McGregors, the only grocery store in town, when a thought occurred to me. I walked next door to the newspaper office and knocked on the half-open door.

"Anybody home?"

I heard running water and soft rock music coming from the back. I pushed the door open and entered a small, messy office littered with coffee cups, dirty ashtrays and piles of books and papers. When I heard the water shut off, I called out again.

"I'll be right out!" a garbled female voice yelled. Shady Sadie, as the locals called her, must have been brushing her teeth.

I had rarely spoken to Sadie face-to-face, although I'd seen her around town quite a bit. On the few occasions that I'd had the chance to get to know her, she'd bottled up, leaving me with the impression that she was something of a snob. But I'd seen her interact with others often enough to know she could be quite charming. Sadie had been running the weekly newspaper for five years now, and her editorializing often infuriated the townsfolk. She was nothing if not opinionated, and I often got a chuckle out of her witty meanderings. She was liberal when it came to politics but staunchly conservative about any proposed changes to the town of Cedar Hills. An avid environmentalist and something of a feminist to boot, she'd ruffled quite a few feathers in the time she'd been here, but what saved her from being run out of town, I thought, was that she always gave equal print to dissenting points of view.

"Sorry, I was just cleaning up," she said, coming around the corner. She was in her late thirties, with long brown hair pulled back in a ponytail and a fresh-scrubbed look that spoke of the early seventies. Her feet were appropriately clad in Birkenstocks, and her Levi's were well faded. If she'd worn a tie-dyed shirt, I wouldn't have been a bit surprised.

"Cassidy James," she said, coming over to shake my hand. "What brings you to my humble abode?" She crossed her arms in front of her chest, leaned back and appraised me brazenly.

I felt an unexpected blush creep up my neck. It had never occurred to me that the infamous Shady Sadie might be a lesbian. But the way she was looking at me made me wonder.

"I was hoping you could help me out," I said, searching for the right words. She continued to gaze at me, and I went on. "I was on my way to put up some fliers around town when it occurred to me that the paper might be an even better way to reach people." I handed her one of the fliers and watched her eyes widen as she read.

When she looked back up, her cheeks were flushed. "What kind of intruder? What does he do?"

"I really don't want to give out too much information. But some weirdo is out there terrorizing women and I want to stop him."

"What do you want me to do?"

"You probably know this town better than I do. What do you think the chances are of someone coming forward with information?"

"What makes you think there's anyone to come forward?"

"Let's just say I have a pretty good idea that this guy has been operating for some time right here in Cedar Hills, and possibly in nearby towns as well. I believe there are women out there who have not reported this crime. I want to appeal to them."

"I don't know." She moved around to sit at her desk and flicked a gold lighter, drawing hard on a filtered Merit. She inhaled deeply. "If someone didn't want to come forward when it happened, I don't know what would make them want to come forward now." She blew smoke rings toward the ceiling.

"That's why I need your help. We need to figure out a way to appeal to their sense of right and wrong. Whoever is doing this has probably not only done it before, but he's going to do it again and again until we stop him. A woman may not come forward for herself, but she might for her daughter or neighbor. That's what I'm counting on."

Sadie looked at me with narrowed eyes, and for the second time that day I felt like a heel. Maybe

Lizzie Thompson was right, maybe I was resorting to emotional blackmail. But unless someone came up with a better idea, it was all I had.

Sadie leaned back in her swivel chair and blew her smoke rings right at me. "Why aren't the police involved in this?"

"Because the person who hired me did not care to involve the police. And if there are people out there who chose not to go to the police in the first place, I'm not sure they'd come forward if the police were involved now. This gives them a chance to help anonymously."

"It might work," she said at last. "At least it's worth a try. Let me see what I can come up with. Why don't you swing back by in an hour or so. By then maybe I'll have something."

I hadn't really intended for her to write an article, but I wasn't going to turn down free help. Relieved, I thanked her and told her I'd be back that afternoon.

Finding twenty-five places to post the fliers in a town as small as Cedar Hills was a challenge. I'd brought a roll of Scotch tape and a pocketful of tacks. I started with the library door and then worked my way across town, hitting the post office, the bulletin board at McGregors, the church, all three bars in town, including Lizzie's, the hardware store, every restaurant, the donut shop and the Elks club, where both the men and women held their monthly meetings. I went to the Cozy Trailer Park and posted one on the bulletin board at the recreation center. I tacked one in the women's restroom at the county dock. Inspired, I returned to the Cedar Hills Lodge and the bars, posting new fliers in the women's restrooms. Maybe with the privacy a bathroom provided, women would feel more comfortable writing down my number.

Finally I was out of fliers. I was also hungry again. Sometimes I think I have a tapeworm. I decided to duck into the lodge for a quick bite to eat before going back to the newspaper office. The lodge has by far the best burger in town, and for some reason a plain old hamburger sounded good.

It was past noon and the restaurant was about half full. I decided to sit out on the front deck at one of the patio tables overlooking the lake. I was not surprised to see Sheriff Booker at another table sitting with a group of businessmen. He routinely worked his way from restaurant to restaurant throughout the week, and his stomach was starting to show the effects. Between his daily lunches and Rosie's cooking, Booker was starting to get a bit of a paunch.

Booker waved me over, scooting his chair to make room for me. I really wasn't in a social mood, but I couldn't think of a polite way to refuse. He was sitting with Mack McKenzie, the mayor of Cedar Hills, and two other men I didn't recognize, but whom I'd seen around town recently.

"Cassidy, your timing's impeccable. We could use a woman's perspective," Booker said, shoving his chair back to stand. The other men stood too, and we exchanged handshakes.

"Of course you know Mayor McKenzie. This is Ned Brand and Pete Sisson. They're thinking of building a new resort in Cedar Hills. Gentlemen, this is Cassidy James, our own local private investigator."

"A private investigator, huh? Imagine that. I

didn't know they had lady detectives," Brand said, sitting back down. He was a tall, hairless man in his early forties. He was light complected and had eyes I didn't trust. He was drinking a Gibson, and he plucked one of the little onions from his glass and popped it into his mouth, grinning like a kid who'd just blown his first bubble. He had an easy smile. Like an alligator, I thought.

The others smiled indulgently and I could have kicked Booker. Normally he'd have made some sarcastic remark if someone had said something that stupid. I couldn't fathom why they were placating this yahoo.

"What do you think of having one of the West Coast's finest resorts right here in Cedar Hills?" Sisson asked. He was large and round with shiny pink cheeks and a reddish handlebar mustache. Like Brand, he had very little hair on his head, and what was there stuck out in little tufts above his ears.

"I don't know," I said. "Does Cedar Hills need a resort?"

"It would sure be a boon to the economy," Mayor Mack said, sipping his iced tea. In his late fifties, he was muscular with a sandy brown crew cut and pale blue eyes. Popular with the ladies for his looks, and with the men for his rugged, tough-guy demeanor, he'd been the popular choice for mayor for nearly ten years. He reminded me of Clint Eastwood.

"How so?" I asked, just to be polite. I really wasn't all that interested.

Just then, Lilly came out to take our orders, and it seemed everyone except me was watching his weight. I listened guiltily as each ordered from the Light Lunch Menu, and I had to refrain from wrinkling my nose at the selections. Even Booker ordered the tuna on plain lettuce with no mayonnaise and a side of sliced tomato. When Lilly looked at me, I practically whispered my order.

"Pardon me?" she asked, smacking her gum. I could have killed her.

"The bacon cheeseburger," I said, giving her my best screw-you look.

"Would you be wanting the curly fries or the regular with that?" she asked, smiling sweetly.

"Regular will be fine, Lilly."

"And to drink?" she asked. I noticed both Booker and the mayor were drinking iced tea, while the two out-of-town big shots were into heavy libations.

"Just a Miller Lite," I said.

Booker looked at me with such envy I nearly changed my order, but by then Lilly had already disappeared. Well, it wasn't my fault he was getting a gut, I thought stubbornly. And it wasn't my fault he was the sheriff and couldn't drink during working hours. At least not with the mayor at the same table. Mayor Mack was something of a puritan. He eschewed alcohol, tobacco and fatty foods. How he survived in Cedar Hills was beyond me. There wasn't a restaurant in town that didn't specialize in deep fried something or other. Every other menu item could have easily been called the Cardiac Special. But Mack was a health nut, and it showed in his robust physique.

"By bringing in new tourists," he was saying, "the proposed resort would positively affect every single business owner in town. The hardware store, the grocery store, the restaurants, the lodge. Hell, even the bars and liquor store would stand to do a booming business. Right now, Cedar Hills is the best kept secret on the Oregon coast. This resort could put us on the map."

As he spoke, both Brand and Sisson were nodding like Kewpie dolls. It sounded to me like the mayor had memorized their spiel.

"What are the drawbacks?" I asked. Ever the devil's advocate, I couldn't resist.

There was an awkward moment of silence, and then Sisson spoke up. "There really aren't any," he said, twirling his mustache. "It's a win-win situation. The town profits and so do we. And, of course, so do the tourists."

"How about the people who already live here?" I asked. "The people who like Cedar Hills the way it is, a nice, quiet lake surrounded by natural beauty? They might not be too thrilled to have their private little paradise suddenly invaded by throngs of tourists. Do people in the town get to vote on this?"

I could tell Booker was starting to wish he hadn't invited me over. The mayor was squirming and Sisson's pink complexion was taking on a reddish hue. It was the mayor who answered.

"Well, now Cassidy. As I'm sure you know, the city council votes on these matters that pertain to zoning and city-owned land. And there will, of course, be town meetings where everyone will get a chance to voice their concerns. But the bottom line is, this town needs this resort. You know as well as I do, or at least you should, that business here is down. People are hurting. It's been a long time since someone has brought in outside money to help bolster our economy. And not only will we reap the benefits generated from the new resort, but part of the deal is that these men are going to dedicate a third of the land to a new public park." The mayor's light blue eyes were lit up and I could tell he was genuinely excited at the prospect.

"I see," I said, trying to sound less critical. I hadn't really intended to rain on their parade. But they'd said they wanted a woman's perspective, and the truth was, I didn't relish the idea of my quiet little paradise being suddenly discovered by the loutish masses. And who needed two parks, anyway? The one we had seemed just fine to me.

I think we were all relieved to see Lilly bang her way to our table. I watched as she set the others' sterile-looking plates, leaving my fat greasy hamburger and fries for last. When she set my plate down, I couldn't help notice Booker eyeing it with envy. I offered him a French fry, but he declined, his eyes mournful as a sulking puppy's.

"Just where is the land for this resort?" I asked, taking a bite of the juicy hamburger.

Booker answered, pushing his tuna around with a fork. "On the north side of Pebble Cove. There's about twenty acres of city-owned land just sitting there. It's got good road access, and it's close enough to town that people camping can just walk right in and buy whatever they need."

"And, of course, the resort will also have its own mini-mall," Brand added, eating his Caesar salad enthusiastically. I noticed he'd ordered another martini too.

"There'll be a laundromat, a gas station, a mini-mart and even a small movie hall. There'll also be boat and Jet Ski rentals, horseback riding, a driving range and a putting green. In addition to full hookup campsites, we'll have fully furnished kitchenettes and a lodge, complete with a real fine restaurant." Both Brand and Sisson were beaming.

"I just wonder," I said, swirling a French fry through ketchup, "with all that right there at the resort, why anyone would ever want to walk all the way into town to do business. And if they don't, then how is having the resort in Cedar Hills actually going to help local merchants?"

Booker looked at me sharply and plucked a French fry off my plate. The mayor's already tanned face darkened noticeably.

"Believe me," Brand said, "just getting people into town is going to help. Sure, they might eat at our restaurant one or two nights while they're here. But the other nights they're going to try out the local spots. Like I said, everyone is going to come out a winner."

I decided I'd played spoilsport long enough. If Booker and Mayor McKenzie were sold on these guys, who was I to find fault? I pushed my plate closer to Booker so he could help himself to my fries without getting ketchup on his sleeve. He scooped up a huge handful and put them on his plate next to the hardly touched tuna.

"Well, it sure sounds interesting," I said, trying to sound cheerful. "How soon is all this going to happen?"

"We're ready to sign papers right now," Sisson said, affectionately twirling the pointed ends of his mustache. "All we're waiting for is the go-ahead from your city council, and we can start clearing. We've already drawn up the plans and have construc- tion crews just waiting in the wings. If things go according to plan, we should be in full operation by next summer."

I didn't know if the gleam in his eye was from sincere enthusiasm or the alcohol he'd consumed before and during lunch. Either way, he seemed to be enjoying himself immensely.

I was saved from having to fabricate more cheerful chatter because Tank McKenzie, the mayor's son, came up to our table and leaned over to whisper something to his father. Tank must have gone to the same barber his dad patronized, I thought, noticing the recent buzz job. He also had light blue eyes and sandy hair, and like his dad, he was clean-shaven. But whereas the mayor looked like Clint Eastwood, somehow Tank seemed more like Tom Arnold. Though only thirty and with the same general build as his father, Tank was already starting to battle a pudgy gut. I watched the mayor shake his head disgustedly and then whisper something back that made the younger man's face redden. Tank turned and left, and Mayor Mack apologized for the interruption.

"I'm afraid there's something I must attend to," he said, pushing himself away from the table. "I trust you gentlemen will find something to amuse yourselves with until this evening's meeting?"

We all stood and shook hands. Booker grumbled something about having to get back to work and I told the men how nice it was to have met them. In truth, it had been an awkward lunch, and I didn't care if I ever saw either of them again. But we all smiled at each other and when I tried to put down some money for my lunch, Sisson waved me away as if he were insulted. Booker walked me out to the parking lot where he'd parked the cruiser.

"Damn," he said, "I never met a more cynical, narrow-minded person in all my life."

"Who?" I asked innocently.

"You know damn well who. I don't know what possessed me to call you over. I should've known you'd take those two sharks to task."

"Hah!" I said triumphantly. "Even you admit that they're snakes."

"I said they were sharks. I never said a word about snakes."

"Same thing. I can't help it if I didn't like them. Besides, you asked for my opinion."

"Yeah, well. Still. You could have shown a little tact."

"You know what I think?" When he didn't respond, I went on. "I think you knew I wouldn't like them, and you knew I'd 'take them to task,' as you put it. I think you wanted me to do just that, because you knew you couldn't very well do it yourself without making the mayor look bad. I think you used me to do your dirty work."

The truth was, I hadn't thought anything of the kind until the words popped out of my mouth, but now that I'd said it, I could tell from his response that I was right on.

"Well, you did bring up a couple of good points, I guess," he said, pretending to smooth his mustache in order to hide his grin.

"You're damn right I did. I'm not at all sure that their little resort would do anything but ruin the peace and quiet of our town." I was embarrassed at the emotion in my voice.

"So it's our town now, is it? It seems to me I can remember a day not so very long ago that you came bouncing into this little town, nothing more than a tourist yourself. Now you want to call it your own and keep it all to yourself." His words would have been cruel if it weren't for the smile he wore. He was making fun of me, but not unkindly. "To tell you the truth," he added, "I'm inclined to agree with you. I don't think we need any more boats and Jet Skis on the water than we've already got. But the mayor sees it differently. And I imagine by this time next week, so will half the town. The vocal half. I'm afraid you better get used to the idea, Cassidy. Cedar Hills is about to become the new favorite vacation spot on the Oregon coast."

Terrific, I thought. But before I could even apologize for having to leave so abruptly the night before or tell him about the fliers, his pager went off and he was gone. Oh, well. He'd be seeing the fliers himself soon enough.

Chapter Five

By the time I got back to the newspaper office, Sadie Long had not only finished her article but also rearranged the entire front page to accommodate it. She showed me her paste-up and my mouth fell open.

"Good God," I intoned. The headline itself was enough to cause a minor panic in town. My reaction made her laugh.

"That's probably what everyone will be saying on Wednesday," she said. Wednesday was the day the *Cedar Hills Press* came out. She handed me the piece and I read it, beginning to wonder if coming to Sadie had been such a hot idea after all.

MADMAN ON THE LOOSE!

Women in Cedar Hills are being terrorized and no one is doing a thing about it! Well, at least up until this week, no one has. But Cassidy James, our own local private eye, is mad as hell, and she's not going to take it anymore! She's going to catch this perverted villain and make him pay! But she needs our help.

If you or someone you know has been victimized by a masked intruder, it's time for you to step forward and help us stop him, before he does it again. And he *will* do it again. This man is sick and cannot stop himself. But with your help, we can stop him before he terrorizes anyone else.

Sadie listed my phone number and stressed the guarantee of anonymity. The piece was awful, I thought, but might just be effective.

When I looked up, Sadie was watching me expectantly. "Well? What do you think?"

"I think we're about to cause quite a shake-up in this little town. I just hope I'm right about there being other women out there. If I'm wrong, we're going to cause a major panic for nothing."

"You're not wrong," she said, flicking her gold lighter to the tip of her cigarette and drawing deeply.

"What do you mean?"

Sadie was looking at the ceiling as she blew

smoke skyward. "I mean, your little idea has already brought somebody forward."

"It has?"

"Yeah. You know, someone who didn't come forward when it happened because the whole thing was too terrible, and she thought it had only happened to her. Someone who now realizes that unless she does come forward, the bastard will just go on doing what he's been doing for the past two years."

Sometimes I think I'm an idiot. It took me an eternity to realize Sadie was talking about herself. At the same instant, I realized I'd never told her the intruder wore a ski mask. How else could she have known he was 'masked'?

"I had no idea," I said, sitting down across from her. My stomach was as knotted as it had been the night before. Sure, I could handle big tough guys with guns, but show me a woman who's been traumatized and I fall completely apart. I borrowed a pen and spiral notebook from the cluttered desk and started to take notes. My hands were shaking. "Two years ago?" I prodded.

She nodded, her face grim. "I'd just written the article on the proposed dam and was taking all sorts of guff over it. The town was in an uproar."

I remembered it well. I hadn't decided for myself whether or not I liked the idea of a dam on the lake until I'd read Sadie's article. I'm sure mine wasn't the only opinion she'd helped form. In fact, I was pretty sure Sadie was instrumental in successfully blocking its construction.

"I'd received some threats on the phone," she said, "but I chalked them up as the price you pay for being vocal. I never dreamed that what ended up happening could ever happen to me."

She took me through it step by step, her voice strangely detached, but her eyes revealing the fear as if it had happened yesterday. There was no doubt in my mind that it was the same man who'd terrorized Lizzie. His basic M.O. hadn't changed, though it did appear he was getting more violent as time went by.

"You say he bound and gagged you. With what?"

She looked at me blankly for a moment. Then her shoulders sagged and she let out a heavy sigh. "He tied me up with nylons," she said, drawing in a deep breath. Her voice was barely audible. "He used my own underpants to gag me."

"Did he say anything to you?"

She nodded, her eyes tearing. "When he first came in the back door, I saw him. He had a ski mask over his head and what I now know was a stun gun in his hand. He waved it at me and told me to turn around. When I tried to resist, he zapped me with the rod, and I was out like a light."

"How did his voice sound?"

"He was half-whispering like he was hoarse. I didn't recognize the voice, and I've been listening for it ever since."

"Which hand was the rod in?"

She closed her eyes, her brows furrowed. "His right," she said. "I'm sure of it. He had on gloves too. I can see it like it happened last night."

It did, I thought sadly. To someone else.

"It was very strange. He seemed more interested in my things than in me. He seemed completely relaxed. He went through everything." She lowered her eyes and stamped her cigarette butt angrily in the overflowing ashtray.

"Did he take anything with him?"

Her eyes shot up at me and her cheeks went suddenly white.

"Come on, Sadie. It's important. What did he steal?"

"It's why I didn't go to the police," she said. "It's such a small town. I really like it here." Her chin had started to tremble, and she looked ready to break down.

"He took something incriminating?"

"A picture," she said, nodding. A tear slid silently down her cheek and she brushed it away angrily. "I should never have kept it. But you don't think about something like that happening, someone going through your things and finding something like that. He stole it. Somewhere, he probably still has it."

"If it's too painful . . ."

"No. It's not just painful. It's ridiculous. I'm a grown woman scared to death that someone's going to think less of me because I'm gay!" She threw back her head and laughed. "Hell! Look at you! Half the town knows you're gay and you could care less."

I wasn't sure what to say.

"The bastard stole a picture of me in the shower with my first and only lover. My college roommate took the picture as a joke and I've kept it all these years, don't ask me why. My lover got married right after college, in case you're wondering." Her tone was bitter.

"Actually, I was wondering why you chose Cedar Hills? It's a lot easier to be out in a big city."

She sighed. "Would you understand it if I told you I've been running away from myself? Living in a backwoods place like this almost allows me to rationalize being closeted. Almost. Like a lot of people, Cassidy, I'm not as comfortable with myself as I'd like to be." She looked away, then slowly brought her gaze back to mine. "Didn't you ever wonder why I've avoided you all these years? You're walking proof that my rationalization is pure bullshit."

What could I say? Sadie obviously had a lot more to deal with than just her experience with the intruder. I nodded, letting her know I understood. "So he found the snapshot and basically used it to keep you silent?"

She nodded, still furious with herself. "I'd have gone to the police if it weren't for that damned photo. And my own stupid hang-ups."

"We all have hang-ups, Sadie. Quit beating yourself."

She looked at me sharply, then relaxed, letting the back of her head rest against her chair. She took a deep breath and exhaled slowly.

"Do you remember what he was wearing?"

"Some kind of light-colored jogging suit. The kind everyone has at least one pair of. Gray I think, or tan." She started to light another cigarette, and then thought better of it. "I've been thinking of quitting," she said. "You know, I hadn't smoked in over a year before it happened. There's nothing quite like being terrorized in your own home to rekindle bad habits. I was up to two packs a day for a while. Just when I thought I was starting to put the whole thing behind me, you show up out of the blue with your damned flier." She let out a short laugh. "For better or worse, you're forcing me to finally deal with this thing. I should have known I wasn't the only one."

"There's no way you could have known," I said. Why was it that victims always seemed to blame themselves?

"I guess I'd convinced myself that it was all mixed up with the article on the dam. I know that doesn't make any sense. But nothing else made any sense either. I mean, why me? Of all people, why did someone choose to do this to me?" She had been fighting tears the whole time but now she let them fall and I knew she was crying for more than just what happened with the intruder.

"I wish there were something I could say or do."

"There is," she said, wiping her eyes. When I looked up, surprised, she smiled. "You can catch this bastard. And let me see him without the goddamn ski mask he hides behind." Her vehemence could have given Lizzie a run for her money.

"I'm afraid you'll have to get in line." I couldn't quite bring myself to smile. "I want to thank you for being the first to come forward," I said, standing up.

"It's I who should thank you," she said. "Weird as it sounds, I feel a hundred pounds lighter." She stood up. "Who knows? Maybe this article will scare up a few more of us. Maybe someone will be more helpful than I've been."

"Oh, but you've been very helpful. For one thing, we know the guy is right-handed, wears sweats and enters people's houses through the back door. And he seems to know his victims well enough to look for something that might incriminate them, to keep them quiet. I do think it would be better if we didn't mention the ski mask in the article, though. Let's

59

hold that little piece of information back for the time being."

Sadie nodded, already crossing out the line.

"By the way," I said. "I may have an idea for another article for you." She arched her eyebrows, and I told her about my lunch with Brand and Sisson and their proposed resort. As I'd suspected, she didn't like the sound of it at all.

"They can't just do that without getting people's input!" she shouted.

When I left, she was already on the phone to the mayor's office, demanding an interview for Wednesday's edition of the *Cedar Hills Press*. Nothing like a new crisis, I thought as I let myself out the door, to help dull the pain of an old one.

Chapter Six

I was anxious to get back home and see if anyone had called in response to my fliers. I knew it was probably too soon, but you never knew. I also wanted to organize my notes and start a profile on the intruder. I hurried back to the marina and when I passed my Jeep Cherokee in its usual spot, I was flabbergasted to see that Tommy had not only washed my car but was laboriously waxing it head to toe.

"Tommy! What on earth are you doing? I was only kidding!"

"R.A.O.K.," he said, grinning at me.

"Huh?"

He was clearly pleased with himself, and in truth, he was doing an excellent job, but still, it made me feel awkward. "R.A.O.K.," he said again, as if I were stupid. "You know, Random Acts Of Kindness."

I continued to look at him blankly.

"Come on, Cass. Don't tell me you haven't heard of it. You're supposed to do nice things for people, and then they'll do something nice for someone else, and then that person will do it for someone else, and pretty soon the whole world is going around doing good deeds. It's the latest craze in California. I'm trying to get it started right here."

"R.A.O.K." I wondered if this meant I'd be obligated to wash someone else's car. Tommy must have read my mind.

"You don't gotta do it," he said. "The idea is, if enough good stuff happens to you, pretty soon you'll feel like passing it on. Anyway, I was gettin' tired of lookin' at this dirty Jeep."

"Well, it certainly looks the best I've ever seen it. Thanks, Tommy."

"No problem, Cass. Take it easy."

I headed back down the ramp to my boat, shaking my head all the way. It sure beat random acts of violence, I thought, but I wasn't at all sure it would take off in Cedar Hills. I wondered how long Tommy's enthusiasm would last if no one reciprocated.

The afternoon wind had come up on the lake, and the usually glassy water was rolling with miniature whitecaps. Even for a Monday, the lake seemed peculiarly deserted. I was ripping along at a good clip, anxious to get home, when I noticed a disabled speed boat off to the right. Someone was standing in the cockpit waving at me like a maniac. I must have been the first boat to come by since the breakdown.

I pulled back on the throttle and made a wide arc, careful not to drench them with my wake. The boat looked familiar and when I pulled up, my heart skipped a beat. The person waving her arms at me was none other than Erica Trinidad. The boat belonged to her recently deceased uncle. She seemed as surprised to see me as I was to see her.

I had to yell to be heard over the wind, which was really gusting. I cut my engine so I could hear her. "What seems to be the problem?"

"I ran out of gas!" she yelled back. "I've got a full can at home, but it's in the other boat. Do you think you could tow me back home?"

I knew my own extra gas can wouldn't be of any use. My Sea Swirl used pure unleaded while her outboard required an oil and gas mixture. I nodded and went to the stern where I kept some tow ropes underneath the seat. I tied one to my boat and tossed Erica the other end. The wind caught it and it landed in the water.

I re-started my engine so I could ease up beside the little speed boat and when the two sides were nearly touching, I told her to hold onto my boat while I went back for the rope. This time, the toss was perfect and I held the boats together while she fastened the tow line to her bow.

"I think you better ride up here with me. You're liable to get drenched back there!" I held the boats steady while Erica climbed into my Sea Swirl.

I took it slow, but even so the little speed boat dipped and bobbed behind us. I wished I could go faster, because having her next to me in the front seat was making me nervous. Neither of us spoke for a few minutes. Finally, Erica laughed.

"What?" I asked.

"I'm not going to bite." She ran a hand through her shiny black hair and gave me a devastating smile.

"What makes you think I thought you were?" I said, thinking I sounded like a two-year-old.

"God, you really hate me, don't you?"

When I looked over at her again, I was surprised to see her eyes watering. Maybe it was the wind. "I don't hate you, Erica."

"You just can't stand to be around me."

"It's not like that." Damn, I thought. She really was crying.

"Then what exactly is it like, Cass?" she asked, turning toward me. She had the most beautiful blue eyes I'd ever seen, and I'd had no idea they could be even more beautiful with tears in them. I was on very dangerous ground and I knew it.

"I'm involved with Maggie now. That's all there is to it."

"You don't think I know that?" she said, voice rising. "I'm not talking about going to bed with you, Cass. I just thought it would be nice if we could be friends."

I didn't know how to answer. We had never really been friends. Nearly every minute we'd spent together had been in bed.

"You and Martha started out as lovers, and she's been your best friend ever since. I don't see why we can't at least be civil?" She sounded terribly hurt.

"Martha and I were never lovers the way you and

I were." I wished I could take back the words as soon as they left my mouth, but like an idiot I went on. "And if I have to explain that, then you're more of a shit than I thought."

We were close to her uncle's place, and I pushed the throttle forward a little, willing the trip to be over. When I felt her hand on my arm, I involuntarily jerked away.

"God, do I repulse you that much?" she asked. The tears were nearly spilling down her cheeks.

"You don't even get it, do you?"

"If you'd just tell me. Talk to me, Cass. Please."

We were about to ram her uncle's dock, and I busied myself with maneuvering the boats so that both would sidle up against it without doing damage to either. The process was a welcome diversion.

Erica hopped out and secured her boat, while I did the same with the Sea Swirl. The wind was whipping around us, making everything more difficult. I helped her untie the tow line, and I stowed it below deck. When I stood back up, Erica was facing me, inches away.

"Tell me what it is I don't get," she said. Her gaze bore into me with such force I could not look away.

"It isn't repulsion that makes me pull away," I said, my voice suddenly husky with emotion. "How can you not know that?"

"You still want me," she said. It wasn't a question.

"No," I said, shaking my head.

"When you're near me, you still want me."

I shook my head, looking down, unable to stand her gaze.

"Right this minute, you want me," she said.

I felt her arms go around me and felt her lips, impossibly soft yet insistent, on mine. My entire body responded, my insides flipping over, my heart dropping like an elevator plummeting. A sob built up inside me from somewhere I didn't know existed, and before I knew what I was doing, I pushed her so suddenly, she toppled. Erica lay sprawled on her back in front of me.

"Erica, I'm sorry." I stood over her, horrified at what I'd done. I felt my knees go suddenly weak. "God, I didn't mean to do that."

"Just go home, Cassidy," she said, refusing to even look at me. "Please, just leave me alone."

I had never seen anyone look so hurt, so devastated, so beautiful in all my life. And I had never felt so low. I got into my boat and raced off, telling myself it was the wind in my face that caused my eyes to tear all the way home.

Chapter Seven

Tuesday morning was bleak. The wind had kept up all night, and now clouds had crowded in and it had begun to drizzle. It was August, for God's sake. It was supposed to be sunny! I was in a foul mood and sensing this, Panic and Gammon were steering clear. Or maybe it was the change in weather that had sent them to curl up on one of the guest beds in the back of the house. Erica's bed, I thought dryly, before she had moved into mine.

I could not get what had happened out of my mind. And I was having trouble separating my emotions. I needed to talk to someone, but I couldn't very well talk to Maggie. Not until I sorted everything out. Booker and Jess were great friends, but they were, after all, men. Lizzie Thompson had enough on her mind without worrying about my little love life. Rick and Towne, the only gay men I knew in town, both would have been sympathetic listeners, but they were off on a cruise in Alaska. That, of course, left Martha, my oldest and dearest friend in the whole world. So why was I hesitant to call her? I knew why, even as I dialed.

"You let her kiss you?" she said, her voice full of incredulity. Up until then, she'd listened without interrupting.

"I didn't exactly let her."

"Oh, yeah. Right." Martha was acting exactly as I had known she would, and it ticked me off.

"If it makes you feel any better," I said, "I sort of knocked her down." This took a minute to sink in.

"You hit her?" She was setting a new world record for righteously indignant retorts. I was starting to regret calling.

"It was more like a push. I didn't mean to. It just sort of happened."

"Let me see if I've got this straight," Martha said. I could just picture her in her office, all duded up in a blue blazer and gabardine pants, leaning back in her swivel chair, her boots propped up on her desk. After she'd been promoted to detective, she'd put her uniform away and spent a whole month's paycheck on new clothes. I could even imagine the tilt of her head as she talked, that little grin on her dimpled cheeks. "You didn't exactly let her kiss you, and you didn't exactly mean to knock her down. Is that about

68

right? Just exactly what was it you were meaning to do, Cassidy?"

"Martha," I said, exasperated. "I know you idolize Maggie Carradine, and you think Erica Trinidad is a complete shit for leaving me, but right now I need you to be my friend, not president of Maggie's fan club, okay?"

There was a brief silence on the other end and then Martha let out a huge sigh. "You're right. I apologize. It's just that I hate to see you screw up what could be a perfectly good relationship with Maggie over someone who has already proven herself to be unreliable."

"That's just it, Martha. I don't want to screw up what I have with Maggie. I just don't know what to do about Erica." I could hear how pathetic I must have sounded.

"Well, I'd tell you to just ignore her, but I guess it's a little late for that. Face it, babe. Erica Trinidad is still under your skin."

"But I don't want her there!" I practically wailed.

"Then tell her so." When I didn't answer, she started to chuckle. "I guess knocking her down was your little way of doing just that, eh?"

"Martha, come on. I didn't mean to push her. It just happened. She's so damned arrogant. Telling me that I want her, and then kissing me like that, and making me . . ." I didn't finish the sentence and Martha pounced.

"Making you what?" she demanded.

"Making me want her more than I ever thought was possible," I said, my heart thudding. I could tell by the creaking sound that Martha had stood up and was no doubt pacing. I think she knew I'd just said aloud what I hadn't even been able to admit to myself until that moment.

"So you want to continue seeing Maggie, except you're still madly in love with Erica? Does that about sum it up?"

"Oh, Martha," I said. "I love Maggie. You know that. I just can't seem to control myself around Erica. All I ever wanted was one woman to love. I'm not like you. I don't need everyone in town to fall in love with me. I never asked to fall in love with more than one woman." Martha started to laugh. "This isn't funny!"

"I know it isn't, babe," she said, still laughing. "I'm not laughing at you, honest." But she was, and I knew it.

"Okay, what then?" I said.

"It's just that for someone so smart, you're so damned dumb when it comes to your own love life. I swear to God, Cass. I wish I could take one of them off your hands for you, but I'm afraid it isn't me either of them wants."

"Tell me what to do. Tell me what you would do."

"Cass, what I would do and what you should do are not necessarily the same thing. If Erica Trinidad, the sexiest woman I've ever seen, and Doctor Carradine, my own ex-therapist about whom I have secretly spent countless hours fantasizing, were both in love with me, I'm afraid I'd be spending an awful lot of time in both of their beds. But obviously that's not your style. I can't tell you what you should do, Cass. But it's obvious you're going to have to decide.

I know one thing's for damn sure. Maggie Carradine is not going to hang around while you make up your mind. She's already made that pretty clear."

It was true. I'd told Maggie that whatever feelings I'd had for Erica were behind me and that I wasn't interested in seeing anyone but Maggie. I'd almost managed to convince her and myself at the same time. I wanted it to be true. The problem was, I was wrong. My feelings for Erica had not died down at all. At least not my physical feelings. They had simply been fermenting, getting stronger as time passed. And now I found myself more confused than ever.

"I just keep hoping this will pass. I don't want to have these feelings for Erica. I want to be faithful to Maggie."

"So be faithful," Martha said in that maddeningly simplistic way she had of viewing the world. "Tell Maggie how you feel and have her help you work through it. She *is* a psychologist, after all."

"She's also my lover. And I want her to remain my lover. I'm afraid that when it comes to Erica Trinidad, Maggie's sense of reason flies right out the window."

By now, all of Martha's other lines were flashing, and she told me if she didn't hang up this instant, they'd be knocking down her door.

"And Cass, about your intruder. I've checked it out and no one's had a case like you've described. Not a lot of help, I'm afraid."

I started to tell Martha about the fliers, but I could hear voices in the background and knew she had to go. I thanked her for listening and hung up, not sure I felt any better at all. But I didn't have a lot of time to dwell on it. No sooner had I hung up from Martha than my phone rang. I had my first response to the flier.

Chapter Eight

"Is this Cassidy James?" the voice asked. It was an older woman obviously trying to disguise her voice.

"Yes, it is. Can I help you?"

"I saw your flier in McGregors. I thought I should call. I don't have much time though. This conversation isn't being taped, is it?"

I assured her it wasn't.

"This intruder of yours, please tell me something about him." Despite her attempt at disguising her voice, she had the distinct air of someone with money. She sounded as if she were accustomed to giving orders.

"Before I do that," I said, "perhaps you could tell me a little about your experience. That way, I'll know if we're talking about the same man."

She let out an exaggerated sigh. "I suppose that makes some semblance of sense." She paused. "The animal who came into my home wore a black ski mask over his face."

It was my turn to let out a gigantic sigh.

"Well?" she demanded.

"Yes," I said. "That fits with the profile of the man I'm trying to find. I know this must be terribly difficult for you and I can't tell you how relieved I am that you've called. If it's all right, I'd like to ask you some questions."

"I assumed as much when I saw the flier. Please proceed."

This was one cool lady, I thought, scribbling as I spoke. "When did this occur?" I asked.

"Last month. July seventh. I'd just returned from the grocery store and was putting things away when I sensed someone behind me. He had what apparently was some kind of electrical prod in his hand and a mask over his head, as I said. He forced me into the bedroom and tied me up."

As gently as I could, I led her through the familiar details, writing furiously. Like Lizzie Thompson and Sadie Long, this woman's hands and feet had been tied with nylons and her underwear stuffed into her mouth. Like the others, she had watched in horror as the man took out what seemed an uncontrolled fury by whipping her bed with a belt he found in the closet. Then he had gone through

74

her things, seemingly unaffected by his outburst. She had refused to tell anyone about the attack, including her husband. Like Lizzie and Sadie, she'd managed to pull herself free. Either the man was lousy at tying knots, or else he wanted them to be able to free themselves after he left.

There were other similarities as well. Again the attacker had been wearing a light colored sweatsuit. He had taken a bath and helped himself to a snack. But most important of all, the caller agreed with Lizzie on the way the intruder smelled.

"He had a peculiarly strong body odor, which he'd tried to cover up with Old Spice. In vain, I might add."

"How do you know it was Old Spice?" I asked, getting excited.

"I just know. I really can't say any more right now."

"Wait. Did you notice any dead animal nearby after he left. A bird, maybe?"

"No. And I've got to hang up." She was whispering, talking fast.

"I can't thank you enough," I said. "Is there some way I can contact you if I have other questions?"

Her laugh was short and dismissive.

"That would hardly go far in assuring my anonymity. If I think of something else, I'll call you."

I was left with the phone buzzing in my ear and a sense of shock. The voice had sounded familiar, even though she'd done a good job of disguising it. The laugh, however, was something I doubted anyone else could have imitated. I'd heard it often enough. The woman who'd just called me was none other than Gloria Baron, the wife of the richest man in town. He was retired now, but she was still active on every committee and council known to Cedar Hills. A powerful woman in her own right, she was made even more so by her husband's substantial wealth.

I went into my study and tore off a large sheet of butcher paper from a roll I kept in the corner. I tacked it to the one blank wall and began to formulate a chart, using a different colored marking pen for each victim. I wrote down every detail of each break-in, even those details that might not have been pertinent. When I'd finished copying the information, I used a yellow marker to highlight the details that were common to all three cases. I then tore off another sheet and tacked it next to the first. At the top I wrote "Intruder Profile." Below that, I filled in what I knew:

Wears light colored sweats
Wears white latex gloves
Noticeable body odor
Uses Old Spice?
Tall, fairly heavy
Enters house through back door
Knows when women do their shopping? (Check with Sadie to see if she was shopping before her attack.)
Disguises voice (someone local?)
Knows his victims? (Hummed Lizzie's favorite song)
Uses some sort of stun gun
Right-handed
Binds them with women's nylons (Why not use rope? Has a thing for nylons?)

Probably intelligent. Knows enough to blackmail victims into silence. Covers tracks
Controlled but angry (Beats the bed, but
  doesn't hurt victims.)
Leaves dead animal? (Was bird a fluke? Or is
  this new?)

I knew there was more, but my neck was starting
to cramp from looking up at the butcher paper. When
I stood back and examined my charts, something
bothered me, but I couldn't quite put my finger on
it. The more I looked, the blurrier it all became and
I knew I needed to take a break. I pulled the shades
in my study, locked the door and slid the key under
a flower vase on the bookshelf in the hall. One thing
I'd learned was that if I wanted to keep something
confidential, I needed to keep it behind locked doors.
There were too many people in Cedar Hills who felt
comfortable barging in on me uninvited.

I'd been avoiding the plastic Baggie long enough,
I told myself. It was time to examine the debris from
Lizzie's drain. I covered the kitchen table with wax
paper and armed myself with tweezers and an
illuminated magnifying glass. Then I began the
grisly task of sorting through the muck in search of
hairs.

I had known all along it wouldn't be easy, but I
wasn't prepared for the difficulty of the job. I started
out with two piles — one for the longer brown head
hairs and one for the shorter, darker, curly pubic
hairs. I'd had no idea there would be so many in-
between hairs to contend with and I ended up with
several piles in front of me.

I wasn't any forensic expert and I knew it. It had been my hope that there among the mousy brown hairs would be one gleaming red or black or blond one that would magically announce the identity of the intruder. But after an hour of eye-straining work, I had to admit that either the guy, like Lizzie, also had brown hair, or he wasn't much of a shedder.

Even so, in the unlikely event that some day a real forensic expert might be able to use them to help nail the creep, I catalogued the hair piles, placed them in separate Baggies and stored them in an air-tight Tupperware bowl. It was a long shot, but it made me feel better.

When I headed into town, it was still drizzling, but not hard enough to necessitate rain gear. I pulled into an empty slip at the marina and the thought crossed my mind that Tommy was probably respon-sible for the weather change. If he hadn't insisted on washing the cars, I mused, we'd probably still be having sunshine. Luckily, he was nowhere in sight, and so was spared from this uncharitable thought.

Between the hardware store and McGregors, a person could get pretty much every necessity for daily survival in Cedar Hills. But for the finer things in life, like clothes and nylons, one needed to go about ten miles south to Kings Harbor. I drove my Jeep through the heavy mist until I reached the Harbor Mall.

BG's was a department store which sold a little of everything. I made my way to the perfume depart-ment and searched among the men's colognes until I found a bottle of Old Spice. I then went to the women's lingerie department and looked over the pantyhose. I had brought one of the nylons the intruder had used to tie up Lizzie, and I was looking for a match. I'm afraid I wasn't very adept at deciphering the pantyhose lingo though. My personal experience with shopping for nylons had been limited to picking up a pack of knee-hi's at the grocery store a couple of times a year. I had no idea there were so many styles, sizes, colors and brands from which to choose.

"Can I help you find something, dear?" an overly made-up woman asked, smiling. She was in her late thirties, which was far too young to be calling me dear. I had to stop myself from replying, "No thanks, sweetie."

"Uh, yes," I said, biting my tongue. "I was looking for these," I held up the pair of pantyhose I'd brought along.

"Well, let's just see," she said, peering at the waistband with disdain. "Why these aren't something we'd carry here. Look, there's not even a label. A person can't even tell which is front from back with these things. If you ask me, they're a waste of money. You get what you pay for, you know. Besides," she looked me up and down with the same lack of regard she held for the pantyhose, "they're much too long for you. Are you sure this is the size you want?"

"Yes." I smiled, gritting my teeth.

She poked around through various shelves before holding up a rectangular package in triumph. "Well, here's the closest thing we've got to *those*. But I'm telling you, they're much too big for you. And the color's all wrong. You'd do much better with a sandalwood tan, or even nude, like this one here with the reinforced toes."

"Uh, where might I find some just like these?"

"Well, I can't say for sure, but I suspect what you've got are L'eggs. You can pick them up pretty much anywhere."

"But not here?"

"Oh, goodness no, dear. I meant anywhere cheap. Although, when ours go on sale, they're not that much more, really. You could probably find a pair across the mall in Pay Less." She wrinkled her nose. "Though why you'd want to, is beyond me."

She was still shaking her head when I walked away and it was everything I could do to not blast her with some witty departing remark. I considered it a Random Act Of Kindness and gave myself a brownie point. I wasn't quite caught up with Tommy, but hey, it was a start.

I had no trouble finding the L'eggs and it only took a few minutes to ferret out the correct size and color. I bought an egg-shaped container of them and left the mall with every intention of going back to Cedar Hills. But, as happened so often, my Jeep insisted on pointing itself toward Maggie's and I had no choice but to go along. It was after noon and I was famished. Maybe I could talk her into taking a lunch break. What I really needed was to talk to her about what had happened with Erica, but I wasn't sure I'd even know how to start.

Maggie's office took up the lower floor of an older house that overlooked the harbor. She lived upstairs and it was there that I hoped to find her. I walked into the downstairs waiting room and was relieved to see there was no one waiting. Her appointments generally started on the hour and lasted about forty-five minutes. It was ten before one. With any luck, she hadn't scheduled a one o'clock appointment.

I tiptoed to her office and listened at the door. There were no voices coming from inside, which was good. Gently, I pushed the door open and peeked into the room. It was possible, I knew, that she had a client with her and they were simply engaged in one of those famous shrink-client silences. I was relieved to see Maggie standing at her window, gazing out at the harbor, no client in sight.

She hadn't heard me come in and I was tempted to sneak over to where she stood and surprise her, but I didn't want to cause a heart attack, so instead I coughed. Even so, she jumped about a foot.

"Cass!" she said, genuinely pleased to see me. "I was just thinking about you."

"I was in the neighborhood," I said. " You look great."

She was wearing a red silk skirt and matching jacket, with a white silk blouse beneath that came close to being translucent. How any of her clients ever concentrated was beyond me. Maggie always dressed to the nines when she was working. I sat on the edge of her desk, admiring her up close.

"Have time for lunch?" I asked, my stomach flipping over nervously. This was going to be harder than I thought.

"I have a client coming in about ten minutes. Unfortunately, I'm booked all afternoon."

She cupped my chin with her delicate fingers. "You okay?" she asked, looking into my eyes.

"Yeah, fine."

I couldn't quite bring myself to look directly at

her. The image of kissing Erica still clouded my mind. Maggie surprised me by leaning over to kiss me. Butterflies took flight as her soft lips found mine and drew me in. It had been a long time since she had initiated anything romantic. For several months, I'd been the one chasing her. Even as I struggled with my conflicting emotions, my heart hammered. I reached around her, letting my fingers trace the firm curve of her hips. Her skirt was short, and I found myself sliding my hands beneath the silky texture.

"Ummm," she murmured, pulling away. "I can't. My client will be here any minute."

"Maggie," I whispered. She stepped back toward me, pressing her lips to my neck, burying her face in my hair. "I want you," I said, my voice suddenly hoarse. Just that fast, my knees had become jelly. The sudden buzz from the waiting room startled us both.

"Damn!" Maggie's face was flushed as she hurriedly rearranged her clothes.

"Can't they wait?" I asked, already knowing the answer. With Maggie, her clients always came first. No pun intended.

"You want to come back for dinner?"

I shook my head. "I need to stick by the phone, but I do want to talk to you."

She arched an eyebrow, but the buzzer sounded again. She shrugged apologetically. "Tomorrow?"

"I'll call you." I kissed her chastely on the lips.

"Don't get me started, Cass. I won't be able to concentrate as it is. I'm afraid you've ruined me for the rest of the day."

"Good," I said, grinning. "Me too."

I let myself out, trying to look like another client

as I passed the woman waiting for Maggie. She was an attractive woman, and for a minute I felt an unexpected pang of jealousy. But Maggie was the consummate professional and would never even think of dating a client. The entire drive home I chastised myself for ever having given Erica Trinidad a second thought, now that Maggie Carradine was in my life.

Chapter Nine

Lizzie was tending bar when I entered the dark, smoky interior of the tavern. There were quite a few men seated around the horseshoe-shaped bar, and others were already working the pool table. Drizzly days had a way of sending all sorts of people to the tavern. When she saw me come in, Lizzie's face clouded over with panic.

"Oh, Cassidy. I'm glad you dropped by. That book you wanted to borrow is in the back." Lizzie was a lousy actress, but the ruse seemed lost on the men. I followed her into a small alcove where she turned on me.

"What are you doing here?" she hissed, eyes like saucers.

"Relax, Lizzie." I said gently, putting my hand on her shoulder. "I've dropped in before, you know."

"But before, there weren't six hundred fliers all over town with your name on them! Everyone is going around whispering about who the intruder is. Worse, they're speculating about who the victims are!"

She had the same wild look in her eyes that I'd noticed Sunday night. I was afraid Lizzie was handling this more poorly than I thought. But she wasn't usually the type to ask for help, I realized sadly. Except she had asked for mine.

I held up the bottle of Old Spice and popped off the top so Lizzie could smell the cologne. She closed her eyes and took a sniff, frowning. Then she took a deeper sniff and her eyes popped open.

"That's it! How did you find it?"

I told her I had already talked to two other women who had most likely been visited by the same man she had, and a look of relief crossed her face.

"And neither one told?" she asked.

"No," I said. "This creep seems to choose victims he knows won't go to the police. It's probably how he's gotten away with it for so long."

As soon as I said it, I realized it was true. And I knew what had been bugging me when I'd studied my charts. I'd profiled the intruder, but not the women he'd harassed. I saw a whole new way of looking at this case.

There was the sudden sound of breaking glass and Lizzie rushed back into the bar. I slipped the Old Spice back into the bag and followed her. By the time I got there, Lizzie had already settled what had apparently been a dispute over who should get up and work the beer tapper in Lizzie's brief absence. The men were looking properly chastised when I let myself out the door.

I walked back toward the marina, thinking about my recent revelation. All of the victims I knew about so far were powerful women in town. But what did that mean? And what else did they have in common, I wondered. Another thought occurred to me. All three lived in houses accessible by car, which in Cedar Hills was not all that common. Many of the houses, like mine, had boat access only. Was this significant, or just a minor coincidence?

I was deep in thought when I practically bumped into Brand and Sisson, the resort enthusiasts. They were walking with Tank McKenzie, the mayor's son, who looked less than thrilled to have inherited tour-guide duty. He smiled at me sheepishly, and stepped off the curb to let me pass.

"You fellows out for a stroll?" I asked.

"On our way to Logger's Tavern," Tank said. "My father said he'd meet us there around four."

I smiled at the two men who nodded in unison.

"That's you who put up the fliers, isn't it," Brand finally said. His alligator smile was wide, but his eyes were wary.

"That's right. Why do you ask?"

"It's just that, well, that's not exactly the kind of publicity that helps get investors interested in committing large sums of money to a town."

"I'm not the least bit concerned about your investors," I said, losing whatever thread of respect I might have had for these two. "I'm concerned about the safety of the women who live here."

"Well, of course," Sisson piped up, clearing his throat. "I think the point you fail to see, Ms. James, is that we're on your side. We want Cedar Hills to thrive. It's just that this is, er, rather unfortunate timing. If perhaps you could just hold off until all the papers are signed..."

I was about to interrupt when I noticed Tank nervously fingering a bulging wad in his jacket pocket. When he saw me look at him, his face turned bright red. I felt my own face flush too, not from embarrassment, but from anger.

"Hand them over, Tank," I said, holding out my hand.

He looked helplessly from Brand to Sisson and then shrugged, digging the wad from his pocket and holding it out to me. My fliers, at least seven of them, had been scrunched into a crumpled blob.

"It was my father's idea," he said, looking mortified. "He was sure you'd understand once we explained."

"Your father may be the mayor, Tank, but he isn't God." I stuffed the wad into my pocket and stormed past them, leaving them gaping after me. If the mayor was upset about the fliers, I thought, wait until he saw tomorrow's headlines in the *Cedar Hills Press*.

Rain had begun to fall in earnest by the time I got home. Panic and Gammon greeted me vociferously, rubbing against me all the way to the kitchen. I was nearly faint with hunger and wasted no time in rummaging through the refrigerator for something of substance. I settled for a bite of cheddar, which I literally bit right off the brick. I grabbed a bottle of Red Dog beer and rewound my answering machine which was blinking rapidly. The first two messages were hang-ups and the third was someone claiming to have been a victim of "my" intruder. It was either a completely bogus call, or we had more than one weirdo on the loose in Cedar Hills. But by the time she got to the part about a green penis, I was definitely leaning toward bogus. The last call was from Booker and he did not sound happy.

"What in holy hell are you up to, Cass? Jesus H. Christ. I've had half a dozen calls already, and everywhere I go, people are asking me what I'm doing about the Cedar Hills Intruder. Only thing is, I can't tell them, since I don't know one damn thing about it. I expect there's a perfectly good explanation for why you haven't shared whatever it is you've got with me. I also expect to hear from you ASAP."

No question about it, Booker was ticked off. Which, of course, he had a right to be. I should've talked to him sooner.

I spent the rest of the evening fooling around in the kitchen and talking on the phone. I finally caught Booker at home and explained what was going on. He was even less happy, after having been screamed at by Mayor Mack.

"These women do not want to go to the police, Tom," I explained. "They want anonymity. I can give them that and you can't."

"But I need to know what the hell's happening in

my own town!" he yelled. I could hear Rosie in the background telling him to calm down.

"I agree," I said. "And if you absolutely promise not to try guessing who these women are, I'd like to share what I know with you."

That seemed to appease him and we agreed to meet the next day for breakfast.

After that I called Maggie but hung up before I'd even finished dialing. I knew I needed to talk to her about the incident with Erica, but I told myself that it was the kind of thing I'd rather discuss in person. In truth, it was the kind of thing I'd rather not have to discuss at all.

Whenever I'm upset, I cook. After everything that had happened the last few days, I was ready for some major culinary endeavors.

Before the night was over, I'd consumed the better part of a bottle of Oregon Pinot Noir, made chicken enchiladas which I sampled and froze, a dozen chicken and mushroom crepes which I also sampled and froze, and an excellent cheddar cheese souffle, a good portion of which I ate. When I went to bed, my stomach was almost in as much turmoil as my mind.

Chapter Ten

On Wednesday the weather was even more dismal than the day before. The Weather Channel said a big storm was heading our way from Alaska, and I couldn't help thinking about Rick and Towne on their cruise ship. But there was enough to worry about right here in Cedar Hills, and more than enough to keep me busy before the big Town Hall meeting at five o'clock.

I'd spent half the morning with Booker, filling him in on the details of the various cases. His expression ranged between incredulity to full-blown fury as I described the intruder's actions. Booker never took notes, but I could tell by the way he was listening that he hadn't missed a single detail.

"If he wears gloves, there's not much chance he's leaving evidence behind," he said thoughtfully, sipping his coffee.

"It doesn't matter," I said. "None of his victims want the police involved anyway. Somehow I think he knows that. He's counting on it."

"But how could he know something like that?" he asked. I hadn't told Booker my theory that all of the victims were powerful women. It would have been as good as giving him names. I sidestepped the issue.

"In a town this small, secrets are almost impossible to keep. What he does to the women is not only terrifying but demoralizing. Also, he's taking something with him that he thinks will keep them from going to the police. He's essentially blackmailing them into silence." I didn't add that while it would be terrible for any woman, it might be even more so for someone in the public eye, whose identity and self-worth revolved around others seeing them as powerful and self-reliant leaders.

"I wish there was something I could do," he lamented. "It puts me in a very awkward position. If they don't come forward, how can I help?"

"Maybe someone will," I said. "After this morning's paper, I'm hoping a few more might speak up."

"You really think the creep lives in town?" he asked.

"It's possible. I think he knows his victims. I think he chooses them carefully. If I tell you why I think that, I'd be breaking the confidentiality I promised." He nodded and I went on. "It could even be someone you and I both know. Probably doesn't look any different than anyone else. He could be married, have kids and hold a regular job. Think about it, Tom. Right now in Cedar Hills, there's someone walking around looking to all the world like a normal, healthy person, who in reality has got some twisted, demented need to dominate, humiliate and defile certain types of women. Maggie says it may well be someone who was himself abused as a child."

"I keep thinking about the grocery store angle," he said. "I don't believe in that much coincidence." The first thing I'd done that morning was to phone Sadie Long to ask her if she'd been shopping right before the attack. Like the others, she'd just returned from McGregors. "Could be someone who works in McGregors," he added.

"I've thought of that. Maybe I should check McGregors' work schedule, see who was working yesterday and July seventh right before but not during the attacks. Somehow, it doesn't seem likely they'd be able to just up and leave when they wanted."

"Unless it was the end of the shift. Maybe there's someone, like a bag boy, or hell, even Roy, the manager, whose working day ended at the same time the women were finishing their shopping."

"But I don't think the intruder is randomly choosing his victims," I said. "It's not enough that they just happen to be shopping at the end of his shift. He knows them. He chooses them."

"Maybe he knows their shopping schedules and arranges his own schedule around theirs."

"Maybe," I said, considering it. "For that matter, it wouldn't necessarily take someone who works in McGregors to know a person's shopping schedule. It could be someone who works on Main Street, who could look out a window and see them drive by."

"Or he could be sitting across the street in Lizzie's bar, looking out the window at McGregors' parking lot. He waits for the right one to pull in, puts his money on the counter and heads out to wait for them at their place."

"It could be anyone," I said, growing frustrated. "Tom, something's been bothering me. Why do you suppose the man uses nylons to tie them up with? I mean, why not just use rope?"

"Maybe he's the type who likes to wear women's underthings." He twirled his mustache thoughtfully.

I looked up at him sharply. Why on earth had he jumped to that conclusion? And why hadn't I thought of it?

"Or maybe he doesn't want to leave marks on their wrists and ankles," he added. "A lot of abusers don't like to leave marks the public can see. I'm worried about that bird, though. Not just that he did it, if he did, but that he hasn't done it before. It could mean he's losing what little control he still has."

"I've been thinking about that. Maybe the bird just flew into the window, Tom. I mean, the step wasn't that far from the kitchen window. It could've hit the window, flown around a bit and then dropped, its neck broken. Maybe the bird doesn't have anything to do with this guy."

"Maybe." He pulled at his mustache. "Let's just hope this article of yours will help scare up some new clues." He patted his copy of the *Cedar Hills Press* which sat on the table between us.

Even though I'd come in to town fairly early, nearly every newspaper stand I passed had been sold out of the paper. As Booker and I discussed the case, I could see the other customers engaged in animated conversations at their tables. Sadie's article on the intruder took up the middle of the front page. Apparently she'd decided it warranted top billing. The remaining space on the front page was dedicated to the proposed resort and Sadie's impassioned plea to residents to come speak out against it at tonight's town meeting. Between the two articles, the whole town was in an uproar.

"I don't suppose you had anything to do with this other article too," Booker said, blue eyes twinkling.

"Now, why on earth would you ask that?" I flashed him my best Miss Innocent smile.

"Just seems kind of funny that Shady Sadie is all the sudden privy to information we just happened to discuss at lunch the other day with those two yahoos."

"Well, you know these journalism types. They seem to have sources everywhere."

"Uh huh," Booker intoned, twirling a toothpick between his teeth. It was obvious he wasn't buying my innocent routine one bit. "As long as you're prepared to be on the mayor's bad side. From what I gather, he's already ticked off royally at you for those fliers. Apparently, not all the promised funds for their little resort have actually been secured yet. He seems to think that news of a 'crazy' loose in Cedar Hills might just scare off the potential investors. I imagine when he reads Sadie's article on the resort and finds out that she's planning on organizing a protest, he's going to really lose his cool. It might behoove you to kind of lay low for a while."

"Well, I sure appreciate the warning," I said, smiling, "but laying low has never been my forte."

"Don't I know it," Booker said, pushing himself away from the table. Obviously his diet had been short lived. I'd just seen him scarf down four pieces of bacon, two fried eggs, a titanic mound of buttery hash browns and a biscuit with gravy. Next to him, my appetite seemed petite.

After breakfast I went for my usual walk through town, making a detour through Lizzie's neighborhood. She'd forbidden me from talking to the neighbors, so there wasn't much I could do. Still, just being in the neighborhood gave me ideas.

Had he just walked down the street and headed straight for her back door? Or had he parked somewhere nearby? Could he be a jogger? The fact that he always seemed to wear sweats made me think he might be an exercise nut. Like me, I thought, looking down at my own sweats.

In fact, I noticed quite a few people in various styles of warm-up suits. There was a man mowing his lawn in a tattered gray sweat suit, two women out for a power-walk in shiny new warm-ups, and a couple of teenagers jogging near the park, one in blue sweats, the other in red. I'd never really noticed before how many locals wore sweats. The intruder probably wouldn't stand out.

But what about the mask and gloves? He obviously didn't walk down the street wearing them. Which meant he'd need a bag of some sort. And large enough to conceal the stun gun.

People didn't jog carrying bags. The more I thought about it, the more I figured he probably drove to the victim's house and parked nearby. Damn! I'd have given anything to question Lizzie's neighbors. But a promise was a promise. I'd just have to find another way.

The wind was still gusty and the temperature had dropped at least fifteen degrees since yesterday. The sky was slate-colored, with some pretty ominous thunderheads skulking in from the north. I'd have bet money we were in for a real gully washer.

Even though I was walking rapidly to keep warm, by the time I'd completed my usual three-mile route, I was chilled to the bone — not just because of the approaching storm, but also because of a growing sense of dread I couldn't quite shake. I felt the intruder was watching me and every time I passed someone on the street, I couldn't help but wonder if he was the one.

I spent the rest of the day in town doing something that made me feel totally ridiculous — pretending to interview people about the article to see if they had any ideas or suggestions on how to catch the intruder. What I was really doing, though, was sniffing men, trying to get a whiff of Old Spice. I knew it was a very common aftershave and that dads everywhere received the foul-smelling stuff on Father's day, and I knew detecting the scent wouldn't mean I'd found my intruder. Still, I felt it was worth a try.

I'd brought the bottle with me and periodically reacquainted myself with its particular qualities, which more often than not sent me into a sneezing frenzy. Several times I thought I detected the cologne, but I couldn't be sure. Ed Beechcomb, the postmaster, was definitely wearing something close to Old Spice, and he had, I knew, once threatened his wife with a butcher knife, upon learning of her vast infidelities. And the post office was just down the street from McGregors, so it was possible he'd have been able to spot his victims heading for the grocery store. Even better, there was no one to watch over him, since he generally worked alone in the post office. He could probably slip out undetected and be back before anyone knew it.

I also thought that Roy, the day manager of McGregors, smelled a bit like Old Spice, but it would have been much harder for him to just leave the store, although even managers had to run errands, I supposed. I was standing about a foot away from him in the small enclosed rectangle that served as his office and thought I detected, beneath the cologne, a hint of unpleasant body odor. But if I sniffed one more time, he would think I was completely looney. As it was, he was eyeing me strangely.

"What can I do you for, Cassidy?" Roy always spoke slowly in his hillbilly twang. He was a tall, lean man in his forties, with light brown hair slicked back off his forehead, making his eyes seem unusually large.

"Well, it's kind of embarrassing, Roy. Can I ask you a favor?"

"Sure can. That's what I'm here for." He gave a buck-toothed grin and folded his arms across his concave chest, like he had all the time in the world.

"Like I said, it's sort of embarrassing. See, there's this man in aisle three, a tall, blond guy with a red shirt on, who I think is following me. He's been walking behind me for several blocks and, well, it may be harmless, but he sort of gives me the creeps. I was wondering if maybe I could hide out here until he leaves."

Roy ran his hands through his slicked-back hair, hitched up his pants and pushed open the door. "You stay right here, Cass. I wanna get me a look-see at this feller myself."

The second he was gone, I searched the small office for the weekly work schedule. I found it on a clipboard hanging from a nail on the wall. It only took a few minutes to ascertain that indeed Roy had been working at the time Lizzie had been shopping in McGregors. I also noted that he'd signed out shortly thereafter. I wanted to find the work schedule for July seventh, but before I could even look around, Roy was back.

"He musta up and left. Ain't nobody out there matches that description now. Still, you can't be too careful these days. You see him again, you let Sheriff Booker know right away. We don't need no hooligans hanging around in Cedar Hills."

I thanked Roy and headed over to Lizzie's tavern, my mind working overtime.

The bar was crowded and I ran into all sorts of people with what I'd call your basic b.o., but not many smelling of any kind of cologne at all. Tommy Greene, who often smelled a little sweaty, used some kind of cologne, but by the time I got to him, my nose wasn't working.

Tommy looked at me strangely when I sniffed him. "You got a cold?" he asked.

"Just the sniffles. It's this weather change."

"Oh. I heard about your masked intruder," he

said, folding his arms across his chest to show off his muscled biceps. All day long, people had been calling him "my" intruder.

"I guess by now everyone's heard. You got any ideas?" I asked, suddenly feeling queasy. Nowhere had the article mentioned the intruder being masked. I'd made sure Sadie left that out.

"I don't know," he said. "What kind of man would do that at all?"

"Tommy," I said, my heart pounding. "Where on earth did you hear that the intruder wears a mask?"

"Well, let's see," he said thinking back. "I think it was that bigwig Brand that mentioned it. I took him and Sisson out to Pebble Cove in the boat this morning. They wanted to look over the property again from the lake."

"What exactly did he say?" I was trying to appear calm despite my racing pulse.

"Well, he was going on about the lousy timing of those fliers and everything, and he said he didn't understand what all the fuss was about anyway, seeing as how the masked man didn't actually do nothing. I just figured he musta knowed what he was talkin' about, he sounded so sure of himself."

This was very strange news indeed, I thought. Either my buddy Tommy was lying to cover up his mistake, or else Brand knew something that only the intruder, his victims, the sheriff and I knew. I felt certain Booker wouldn't have told anyone. Nor would Lizzie. And unless Sadie had changed radically since yesterday, I doubted she had told a living soul. That left the mysterious caller, whom I figured to be Gloria Baron, and whoever else might have been victimized by this creep. And of course, the creep himself. Not for the first time I wished I knew which victims had gone to Maggie. Had it been Sadie or Gloria Baron? Or were there others out there I hadn't even heard from?

I pictured Ned Brand and tried to imagine him as the intruder. But Sadie had been attacked two years ago. Could Brand have been in town back then? Maybe scoping out the area for his proposed resort? Perhaps it had taken him a full two years to get the needed financial backing to finally pursue his dream. One thing was certain, I'd need to find out. But who would know? I doubted Brand himself would be up-front about being here if he were the one breaking into women's houses. But maybe Sisson could confirm Brand's presence in Cedar Hills two years ago. On the other hand, maybe it was Sisson who was breaking in. Maybe he'd been the one to bring up the mask to Brand. Hell, as far as I knew, it could be Tommy. No, that wasn't possible, I thought, shaking my head. By the time I got home, I was not only confused but exhausted.

I hadn't expected there to be such an immediate response to Sadie's article, but my answering machine was going crazy. Panic was standing over the phone in her attack stance, as if ready to pounce on the next caller. I hit the rewind button and then listened, taking notes as I did. When the tape was finished, I replayed it again and again until I practically had the messages memorized. Two of them, I was pretty sure, were authentic.

The first call had been from a woman who claimed to have been "burglarized" less than a week ago. She gave enough information to convince me that she'd been attacked by "my" intruder. And best of all, she had one detail that none of the others had mentioned.

"I think he's bald," she said. "When he grabbed me, I tried to fight back. I grabbed the mask covering his head and tried to pull his hair, but I couldn't feel any. Then he shocked me with something like a cattle prod and there was nothing I could do."

Other than that, her story had been nearly identical to the others. Unfortunately, she hadn't left her name and I didn't recognize the voice at all.

The other calls were an assortment of well-wishers and curiosity seekers. And one, I was pretty sure, was a false confession. But it was the last call that sent chills up my spine. No wonder Panic had been in her attack stance. He must have called right before I came in.

"Hello there," the voice said. It was a soft whispery voice, clearly being disguised. "I hear you're looking for me. Well, don't look too hard. You're likely to find me sooner than you think. In fact, you never know when I might just pop in the back door. Well, gotta go. I'll be seeing you."

The hair was standing up on the back of my arms and neck. I went to my bedroom closet and checked my Smith and Wesson .38. Feeling somewhat ridiculous, I strapped on my shoulder holster and went around the house doing something I very rarely did; I locked the doors. Then I let myself into my locked study and worked on my charts until my head ached.

Chapter Eleven

I'd asked Maggie to meet me at The Cove for dinner. Too expensive by Cedar Hills standards, The Cove was miraculously still in business after two full years. It was a small restaurant, with about a dozen tables overlooking the lake. It was only open for dinner and served a very limited prix fixe menu. It was by far my favorite place to eat in town.

"Goot evening, Ladies. Jour table is vaiting for you. And I haff a veddy nice vine for jou tonight. Veddy dry, zee vay jou like it."

"Thank you, Pierre," I said, sinking into a plush

chair across from Maggie. I was pretty sure Pierre was from the Midwest and only faked the accent, but I'd never let on I knew.

"Jou vant zee escargot, or zee pâté platter for zee first course?"

Snails are not my thing. We ordered the pâté.

Maggie was wearing a simple black turtleneck and gray slacks that might have looked plain on someone else. On Maggie, they looked elegant. Her green eyes caught the candlelight and seemed to dance.

"So, you've stirred up quite a hornet's nest," she said after Pierre brought the wine. It was a French Merlot, and dry as promised. I told her about the latest happenings and she listened intently. "This could be very dangerous for you, Cass. If he sees you as a threat, he's likely to come after you."

"That's why I brought this." I pulled back my jacket and showed her my shoulder holster, my .38 nestled comfortingly inside.

Maggie shook her head. She didn't mind scaling mile-high precipices with her bare hands but worried that I might get hurt as a P.I.

"You should have been a mother," I teased. "You have great maternal instincts."

"I'm not mothering you. But I do wish you'd be a little more cognizant of the dangerous situations in which you seem to enjoy placing yourself. Sometimes I think you thrive on it."

"Kind of like you do? Honestly, Maggie, anyone who wants to go bungee jumping must have something a little haywire, don't you think?"

Pierre brought us a small plate of pâtés and a basket of crusty French bread. Maggie ignored my comment.

"So you're hoping to provoke him?" she asked, daintily spreading the liver on a thick hunk of sour-dough.

"If I get the chance. I just can't shake the feeling that he's right here in town. That he's watching me. It's an unfair advantage. I want to make him show his hand. Lessen his advantage."

"Just hope the hand he shows you doesn't have a stun gun in it." She smiled wryly.

As Pierre brought out successive courses, our conversation moved lightly. I tried several times to bring up what had happened with Erica, but the time was never right. Finally, Maggie brought it up herself.

"You've got something on your mind, Cass. Why don't you just come out with it?"

"What makes you say that?"

She laughed. "Your face is an open book. It's one of the things I like about you. So what is it? Something to do with Erica Trinidad, right?"

"Maggie, I can't believe you."

She waited patiently.

"I ran into her the other day. On the lake. Her boat was out of gas and I towed her back to her place."

"Uh huh." There was no criticism. Just patience.

"She kissed me," I blurted out. "And I sort of pushed her down."

"You pushed her?" So much for a shrink's objectivity, I thought.

"It was a completely unplanned reaction," I said. "I've never done anything like that in my life. Well, except on a case when I was being attacked. But never a woman. Never someone I cared about."

"So you're finally admitting you still care for Erica."

"That's not what I meant. I mean, of course I still care for her. You can't just turn something like that off. But, well, I didn't want her to kiss me." I knew I sounded pathetic. I could hear the defensiveness in my voice but couldn't stop it.

"People don't ordinarily get violent with someone who tries to kiss them, Cass. There are other, less dramatic ways of telling them you're no longer interested in their affections." Her eyes bore into mine and I looked away feeling my cheeks redden. "Unless of course, you are still interested in her affections and you're really angry at yourself for feeling things you don't want to feel. I mean, if you're really fucked up about it, I can see where you might end up turning your anger on them." Maggie rarely cursed and when I looked up, there was anger in her usually calm eyes.

"Maggie, please. I need you to understand."

"I do," she said, pushing herself away from the table. "Obviously, I understand you quite a bit better than you understand yourself."

I watched her leave, feeling at a total loss. I could run after her, but what would I say? What she said was true. I did still care about Erica. I could no longer deny it, even to myself. I put some money on the table, leaving Pierre an obscenely large tip, and let myself out of the restaurant feeling miserable.

Chapter Twelve

The only place big enough to hold a town meeting was the old Methodist church. When I got there, the place was already packed with people standing in the aisles and spilling out the door. Mayor Mack was standing at the podium, banging a gavel. I squeezed my way through the crowd and found Booker, who had promised to save me a seat. True to his word, there was a vacant spot between him and Jess Martin. Lizzie Thompson was on Booker's left and as I sat down, I saw practically everyone in town I knew.

"I'm thrilled to see such a terrific crowd here tonight," the mayor said loudly into the microphone. Most of the talking died down and he lowered his voice. "As you know, we are very honored and excited to have with us this evening two distinguished gentlemen who have plans to finally put Cedar Hills and Rainbow Lake on the map."

There was a smattering of applause, but quite a bit of grumbling too. I was surprised to see Sadie Long sitting next to Gloria Baron and found it ironic that neither woman knew the other had been through the same terrible ordeal.

"As many of you know," the mayor went on, "business has been down in Cedar Hills ever since they passed the restrictions on salmon fishing. Most people don't even know we're here. Thousands of tourists drive by each year and stop ten or twenty or thirty miles up the road, spending their money elsewhere. But it doesn't have to be that way. And here to tell you how we can change all that is a man I know you're going to love, Ned Brand!"

There was polite applause as Brand took the stage, but quite a few townspeople, including those closest to me, seemed to be reserving judgment.

Brand's cheeks were rosy, and even from where I was sitting, I could see the gleam in his eye. I wondered idly how many martinis he'd had with his lunch.

"So happy to be here," he was saying. "This is such a lovely little town, and it's so exciting to discover so many honestly good people in one place."

He was obviously trying to butter us up, and from the nodding heads, it seemed to be working. He went on about this being the chance of a lifetime, and how marvelous it was to be able to envision something that would bring prosperity and wealth to our community. When he'd exhausted every conceivable benefit of the new resort, he brought on his sidekick, Sisson, to describe the glorious resort itself.

Sisson seemed unusually nervous, and I noticed his shirt was beginning to soak through with perspiration beneath his armpits. He smoothed his pointy mustache and coughed into the mike. When the crowd had finally quieted, he began to speak in a soft voice. Despite his obvious nervousness, he was an impressive speaker. Using colorful imagery, he painted a vivid picture of a fabulous resort. I had to admit, even I was impressed with the magnitude of their proposal. When he finished, there was genuine applause.

Mayor Mack took the microphone again, his face beaming. "Let's show these gentleman what a real Cedar Hills reception is like!" he said, facing the two men and clapping like crazy. The crowd responded, and it seemed that the resort would be a done deal.

"I have a question!" I heard Gloria Baron say in her regal, imperious tone. The noise died down and the mayor looked at her politely.

"Yes, Mrs. Baron. We're always glad to hear from you."

"Just what will the added boats do to the quality of the water that most of the people living out on the lake use for drinking water? Has that been addressed?" There was quite a bit of head-nodding and murmuring.

"Well, er, I don't see how a few more boats will make much difference in a lake this size," Brand said.

"But you yourself said the resort would bring in thousands each summer!" someone shouted.

"And what about all the cars?" another voice yelled. "Next we'll be needing traffic lights in town."

The mayor took the microphone from Brand and waved his arms like a quarterback quieting his home crowd.

"All of these are valid questions and believe me, I've considered every angle of this proposal. Traffic for the resort will be re-routed so as not to jam our main streets. Most of the tourists will be in R.V.'s, and will be walking into town once they're situated in the resort. The resort itself will be renting boats with electric motors rather than gas-powered ones, so the water quality should not be affected in the least."

"But what about all the people who bring their own boats?" Sadie Long asked, standing up. "Are you saying that soon you'll want to regulate the type of boat anyone can use in the lake?"

"Of course not." The mayor was starting to sound perturbed.

"Then how can you guarantee that the water quality won't be tainted?" Sadie demanded.

Before he could formulate an answer, Susie Popps, a vivacious real estate agent, stood up and walked to the stage, taking the microphone from the mayor.

"You're all missing the point!" she said. The room grew silent, and Susie went on, gesturing for emphasis.

"You all are being sold a bill of goods." She looked pointedly around the room. "Mayor Mack is telling you this will be good for the town. Business will pick up because the tourists will be bringing their hard-earned money to spend in Cedar Hills. But the truth is, they'll be spending it at the resort. These two men have made a great sales pitch, and I think some of us almost fell for it. But think about it. They've got their own laundromat, their own gas station, their own mini-mart, their own fancy-dancy restaurant, their own bait shop, their own boat rentals. What in the world would any of them need to come into town for? All they're going to be using that's ours is the lake. That means strangers will be racing around on Jet Skis and water skis and speed boats, throwing their litter in the lake, not giving a darn about those of us who live here. Boating accidents will be up, and the peace and quiet will be gone. Who will benefit from this resort? Not me. Not the store owners. Not the restaurant owners. Not the hardware store. Not the marina owners. Not even the gas station! The only ones who will benefit from this resort will be the rich tourists who descend on us in droves, and these two gentlemen who will get richer than they already are. For the life of me, I can't figure out why Mayor Mack is trying to shove this down our throats, but that's the way I see it."

The burst of applause was cacophonous, and Mayor Mack's face had turned a startling hue of crimson. I could even see a blue vein pulsing beneath the surface of his neck.

Gus Townsend, who was on the city council, stood up and shouted over the noise. "I, for one, am with Susie. Let the record show that my vote is against this proposal."

"Now, Gus," McKenzie said, having wrested the microphone from Susie. "This is not the time for a formal vote. This is simply a time to discuss the issue and get answers to the questions and concerns that some people might have."

"I vote against it too," Gloria Baron said, standing up. "And I think this a very fitting time for a vote."

"You can count me out as well," Sam Pratt said. "I agree with Susie. This whole thing seems to be being shoved down our throats and I'm not even sure why. Besides, I drink that water. I don't want any more boats on it than what we already got. My vote is no."

Just like that, the other council members voiced their concerns and voted against the proposal. Mack's face looked almost purple. I wondered if anyone in the room was trained in CPR, because it appeared a coronary wasn't completely out of the question. Brand and Sisson seemed likewise stunned at the turn of events. The three of them stood helplessly on the stage, mouths agape. They were saved from having to admit defeat by a female voice from the back of the room.

"Now that that nonsense is out of the way, what about this intruder?"

The whole room exploded again in shouts and I heard several people calling my name. I stood and made my way to the stage, trying to avoid the mayor's eyes which were glowering at me with undisguised fury. It wasn't my fault the town had vetoed his pet project. Why was he so ticked off at me? I took the microphone as the three men stomped off the stage.

111

"For those of you who don't know me," I said, "my name is Cassidy James. I'm a private investigator, and as many of you do know, I'm trying to find the man who has been terrorizing women in our town for some time. There may be women here tonight who could help me with this investigation, but who are ashamed or afraid that somehow their names will be used. Let me assure you right now, anyone who talks to me will be guaranteed complete anonymity." The room was so quiet I could hear the ticking of the clock on the back wall. "This intruder is a coward. He likes to terrorize women when they're helpless to fight back. And he hides behind a mask. He may be married, may even have children. In fact, someone in this room right now may be married to him and not have any idea what he's doing."

There were several gasps, and I could feel people squirming, but their eyes were riveted on me.

"He probably looks and acts as normal as everyone else except, of course, when he's breaking into women's homes. That's why you shouldn't be ashamed if you begin to suspect that someone you know may be the intruder. It's not your fault that you didn't know. How could you? He's an accomplished liar. He has secrets and he's good at keeping them. We think we know what kind of cologne this man wears. Old Spice. We also know that this man uses some kind of electrical device, like a stun gun or maybe a cattle prod." There were several gasps but again the room fell silent. "He's right handed. He wears light-colored sweats. He uses white latex gloves. He's fairly tall. And while he's outwardly controlled, he also has quite a volatile temper. He may also have an unusual body odor."

There were a few chuckles, but they died down quickly.

"There is a great deal more we know about this man, but I don't want to show all my cards just yet. What I do want is to ask every single person in this room to think hard. I'm going to give you three dates and times and I want you to write them down or remember. Because someone in this town was invading women's homes at those times. And if someone you know cannot be accounted for on all three of those dates, then I am begging you to come forward. I know this will be difficult. Nobody wants to admit that someone they like, or even love, could be this intruder. But not only do I think that this man may live right here in Cedar Hills, I believe he may be right here in this room."

A murmur erupted immediately and tension filled the room.

"How do you know!"

"Who are you to accuse people?"

"What can we do?"

The voices came from all over and I did my best to quiet them down. Then I gave the three dates and times, repeating them several times. "Ask yourself, is there someone I work with who left early on those dates? Ask yourself, was my husband acting strangely on those dates? Ask yourself, does someone I know possibly fit the profile of this man? If the answer is yes, I beg you to call me."

I glanced at Booker and he nodded reassuringly. I knew I was taking a chance by giving out so much information, but I was about to go even further. "At this time, I'd like to ask all the men to leave the room."

There was a shocked silence.

"It will only be for a minute," I went on. "Please. There's something I'd like to share with just the women."

It was interesting to watch the awkward procession. Some of the men laughed nervously. Others grumbled. Still others seemed anxious to get out, relieved to be set free. When the room was finally empty of men, I walked to the edge of the stage, leaving the microphone behind me. When I looked up, I was surprised to see Maggie standing in the back against the wall. She smiled and my throat constricted. I spoke so softly several women had to lean forward to hear me.

"I know nobody here wants to believe that a husband or boyfriend or son could be the same man who is terrorizing other women, but the truth is, there's a very strong possibility that someone, maybe several of us in this room, are quite close to this man. And I also believe that there may be women in this room who have been harassed by this man but have not told anyone because they felt ashamed or afraid. I can only tell you that you are not alone. And the shame is not yours, it is his. It is no crime to be a victim. I'm going to tell you something I did not want to say in front of the men. Because if you are living with, or are close to this man, you may be in some danger if he knows that you know about this next detail. I'm asking you to keep this next item between us women for now."

"What is it?" Susie Popps asked impatiently.

"The man we're looking for may like to wear women's underclothes, particularly nylons." I still wasn't at all sure I believed this, but I didn't want to ignore the possibility. "At the very least, he seems to have an unending supply of pantyhose, and they're large enough to fit a tall man. By the way, this is the same brand and size he's left behind." I held up the L'eggs container and passed it around the room. "He may be taking them from his wife's drawer or he may buy his own. Either way, he probably has a secret place he keeps them, along with the stun gun and the things he takes from the women he visits." I paused. "So I ask you to think about it. Does your husband have a secret, private place that he keeps locked up? Does he seem to have a fixation with nylons? Has he ever asked to tie you up with nylons, or asked you to tie him? And has he ever beaten you with a belt? Or threatened to? Or beaten another object in the room when he was really angry with you?"

There was an uncomfortable silence hanging in the room. Heads were shaking, most women obviously relieved that the description did not implicate their men. But not everyone was in agreement.

Suddenly, Wanda Pearson, who ran the donut shop, stood up. "He came into my home," she said. There was a stunned silence and she went on. "I never told anyone. He came in with a ski cap over his head and he, he, tied me up, and he, he, it's too awful!" Women were staring at her with a mixture of shock and compassion.

"When was this?" I asked.

"Just two weeks ago," she said, breaking down. It was beginning to look as though the intruder's pace was definitely escalating.

"I was attacked too," Janet Sawyer said, getting to her feet. "I was going to call the police, but I was too ashamed. He cut all my underwear to shreds. I couldn't even tell my husband, but now I'm going to. I thought I was the only one. I was afraid he'd come back!"

Women in the room had tears in their eyes, myself included.

To my surprise, Sadie Long stood up. The whole room fell silent as she spoke. "I was terrorized two years ago and I never told a soul. But it's the same man. According to Cassidy, he hasn't changed at all. Except he's getting worse."

Women were looking around the room expectantly. It was beginning to resemble an AA meeting, which was not at all what I had intended.

"You are very brave, all of you, for stepping forward now. But, ladies, please don't feel that you have to. You can call me, if you prefer. I know how hard this must be."

"No, you don't, Cassidy." It was Lizzie. "You can't really know unless it's happened to you." Her voice was thick with emotion. "The bastard attacked me a few days ago. I'm the one who called Cassidy," she said, her voice breaking. "I didn't have the guts to go to the police. I was afraid of what people might think of me if they knew what I'd been through. I didn't want pity. I didn't even have the guts to tell Cassidy everything the bastard did. But I'm not afraid any more. I'm just plain mad." Even from the stage, I could see the fierce resolve in her eyes.

What happened next was truly amazing. The women who had spoken out had all remained standing, and now the other women gathered around them, exchanging hugs and offering their support. It was a bit like being at a funeral, I thought. There was a sense of bonding that seems to only occur in the wake of some tragedy. It may have been anti-climactic, but I felt we needed some closure. I glanced at Maggie and she nodded approvingly. She was far better equipped to handle this kind of thing than I was, but it was my show and I'd just have to do the best I could. I was good at getting people riled up. I wasn't sure how adept I was at getting them calmed down.

"Before we go," I said, "I need to warn you that this man seems to be rapidly escalating his activities. Now that I've ridiculed him by calling him a coward, he may be even angrier than before. And I believe he is plenty angry already. Please be careful. Lock your doors and take someone with you when you return home from shopping. For some reason, he likes to attack women in their homes after they've been to McGregors. And please, if you can think of anything at all that might help, call immediately. If you suspect someone you know, be it your husband or son or whoever, don't confront them. Call me."

Outside, the men were waiting for us, worry and curiosity etching their faces. I saw Booker and headed toward him, but Mayor Mack blocked my path.

"I hope you're happy," he snarled. "In just one day you've managed to ruin whatever chances this town had of making something of itself, and now you've got everyone running scared. There's not a woman in town who can trust her own husband, the way you put it. I guess you'd be happy if every woman were another man-hating dyke like you."

"Dad, knock it off," Tank said, coming to stand beside his father. He looked totally mortified at his father's vehemence.

"I'm sorry you feel that way, Mayor. I can assure you my only concern is for the safety of the women in this town. I would think that would be your main concern too."

"What *I* think is that you're so busy mountain-climbing mole hills, you can't see the damage you're doing to this town." The little vein beneath the skin of his neck was pulsing dangerously.

"Dad, she's just trying to help. What if it were Mom? If you look at it that way..." He didn't get a chance to finish. His father shot him a withering look and he quickly closed his mouth.

"When I want your opinion, I will ask for it," he hissed. He pushed Tank aside, and stormed off in the direction of his car.

"Sorry about that," Tank said, studying his shoes. His face had reddened at the insult from his father and I felt sorry for him. It couldn't be easy living in the shadow of such a forceful man.

"It's okay," I said. "I know he's really just upset about the resort. Speaking of which, do you happen to know when Sisson and Brand first became interested in Cedar Hills? Someone said they've been planning this for quite a while."

"At least a couple of years now. I remember, they were here back when that dam was being proposed, and they wanted to see how that was going to come out before they went forward. Now it looks like they've wasted a lot of time for nothing. My dad pretty much convinced them that the town would love the idea of the new resort. I don't think he had any idea people would respond the way they did tonight."

"Well, you don't seem too upset about it," I noted.

"To tell you the truth," he said, tugging his earlobe, "it's kind of nice to see him lose for once. But don't tell him I said that." He smiled sheepishly and moved off in the same direction as his father. I looked around for Brand and Sisson, wondering where they had disappeared to, when I felt someone at my elbow and turned to see Maggie's lovely eyes.

"You did fine," she said. "And I apologize for acting like such a moron. I had no right to walk out of the restaurant like that, no right to talk to you that way." When I started to answer, she put her hand on my arm. "Listen, some of these women may need counseling, Cass. This wasn't the time or place, but I'd like to offer my services. This guy has obviously done some serious psychological damage. Call me and we can figure something out." She turned to go.

"Maggie, wait." I walked with her away from the crowd. "About what you said earlier. You were right. Obviously, I have some things I need to work out. But that doesn't change how I feel about you."

"I know that, Cass. It's just that it limits how I'll allow myself to feel about you. That doesn't mean we can't still be friends. Give me a call."

I watched her go, trying to swallow the lump in my throat.

Chapter Thirteen

That night I slept fitfully, waking at the slightest noise outside, three times getting up to prowl the house, check locks, peer out into the moonless dark for would-be intruders. It was in the wee hours of pre-dawn when I finally succumbed to sleep and even then, my dreams kept me from really resting.

In one, Maggie and I were walking in the woods. The huge trees towered over us, their scented needles nearly obliterating the sun. We were holding hands, taking in the natural beauty as we walked along the pebbled path. Suddenly, Maggie's beeper went off.

"Damn," she muttered.

"Can't it wait?" I pulled her toward me, but her green eyes narrowed and she shook her head.

"I have a client who's on very unstable ground," she said, already turning back. "Just wait for me down by the stream. If I'm not back in fifteen minutes, I had to go."

"But," I started, watching her vanish around a bend. For some reason my feet seemed rooted to the ground and I was unable to follow her.

Frustrated, I continued down the path toward the gurgling stream. I was getting closer and the sound of running water was making me unbearably thirsty. I started jogging.

When I rounded the last bend, I came to a jolting halt. There, next to the stream on a white satin blanket, was a woman sitting cross-legged with her back to me. She was wearing a royal blue silken robe loosely belted, one bronze shoulder partially exposed to the dappled sunlight.

My heart unexpectedly began to pound, and my mouth, already parched, ached with the need for moisture. I was about to bolt when she turned and my heart plummeted. The woman was Erica Trinidad.

She smiled provocatively and patted the satin blanket beside her. I shook my head, taking a fearful step backward.

"Come here," she said, her voice low and sensual. "I have something for you."

Still, I stood my ground, shaking my head.

"I have what you want," she said more forcefully. Her robe had fallen open, exposing one voluptuous breast, the bud of her nipple standing impossibly erect. I gulped, barely able to swallow. She laughed and reached into a straw-colored basket, bringing out a plump coconut, carved open and brimming with its own juices. She held it out to me, an innocent offering.

Tentatively, I made my way to the blanket and found myself kneeling before her. She would not fully relinquish the coconut, but rather held it for me while I drank greedily, my hands covering hers.

There seemed no end to the juice in that coconut and I drank insatiably. When at last I'd had my fill, I pulled my lips away. They were ringed with milk and Erica reached up to wipe it away with her fingers. When she put her fingers between her own lips, I moaned with longing.

"Here," she said. She took her finger and swirled it around the inside of the coconut, then placed her fingers to my lips. I surprised myself by sucking hungrily. My eyes were closed; I was intent on drawing out every ounce of succulent moisture from her fingertips. When I opened my eyes, I was shocked to see that she had inserted her breast into the open coconut, and when she removed it, it too was laced and dripping with white.

Obediently, I moved my lips to her breast, devouring every bit of moisture as if I were dying of thirst. I was lost in an insatiable need, and it seemed that the more I drank, the thirstier I became. I was moaning with both need and pleasure, and so could barely hear the sounds coming from Erica.

Finally her husky words broke through. "Here," she said, "drink from here."

I looked up to see that now her robe had fallen completely away, and my heart flipped over dangerously. She touched her thigh, letting her fingers trail languorously toward the point in question.

My throat constricted, the longing so deep and unbearable that I nearly choked with desire. As I moved down, letting my hands brush her satiny skin, I heard the sudden, incessant beep of Maggie's pager. I struggled to break free from the passion that had nearly engulfed me, and when I finally did, I realized the phone was ringing.

Chapter Fourteen

"Susie Popps is dead."

"What?" The phone had pulled me from the depths of the dream and my heart was racing.

Booker's voice was haggard. "The neighbors heard screaming last night. By the time I got there, she was already gone."

I looked at my clock. It was barely six a.m. "How?" I croaked. "Where?"

"I'm afraid it's your intruder, Cass. Looks like last night he finally went over the edge."

My mind was reeling. He meant that I had sent

him over the edge with my speech. I was responsible for Susie Popps' death. Suddenly I felt sick to my stomach.

"How did she die?"

"Stabbed. Coroner from Kings Harbor estimates at least thirty times. Martha's here, been here since three. This time, he may have left some evidence."

"Where are you?" I said. "I'm coming over."

"There's nothing here for you to see, Cass. I just didn't want you to hear it from someone else."

I knew what he was saying. Within the hour, everyone in town would know what had happened. And they'd all know just exactly who had pushed the man over the edge to murder.

"Shit!" I said.

"My sentiments precisely," he agreed. "Listen, I'm sending Martha over to your place. You may be in some danger."

"From whom?" I asked, my voice icy. "The killer, or the people of Cedar Hills?"

"Now, Cass," he said, sounding tired. "I knew you'd be like this. It isn't your fault. From what you've told me, this guy has been decompensating rapidly. It was bound to come to this. Besides, I think I know why he killed her. I mean, I don't think he went in there planning to do it."

"What do you mean?" When he didn't answer right away, I repeated it. I was desperate. He took a deep breath.

"I think she saw him and recognized him. He couldn't leave her alive."

This was Booker's way of handing me a life-ring. I grabbed it and held on with everything I had. "How do you know?"

"Three of the nylons he used to tie her up were still tied to objects in the room. But one she'd managed to pull free from the bedpost. Guess what she had clutched in the hand she'd managed to pull free? A black ski mask."

"You think she broke free, grabbed the mask off of his head, and that's why he killed her?" The relief I felt was immense. Maybe it wasn't my fault. Please God, I thought, don't let Susie's death be my fault.

"He never killed before, Cass. Something had to happen to make him cross the line. Maybe he was escalating, and maybe last night's talk got him charged up, but if Susie hadn't seen his face, I believe with all my heart that she'd be alive right now."

But if I hadn't gotten him "charged up," I thought, maybe he wouldn't have gone to Susie's at all.

"I sent the cap to the lab to have them check for hair follicles. I checked as well as I could myself and couldn't find a thing. You'd think if he'd had the cap over his head and she pulled it off, then there'd be at least a hair or two inside."

"Not if he's bald," I said.

"What?"

I told him about my latest caller who'd said she thought her attacker may have been bald.

"Jesus H. Christ!" he yelled. "Why didn't you say so sooner?"

"And, Tom," I said, ignoring his outburst, "according to Tank McKenzie, both Sisson and Brand were in Cedar Hills two years ago when that business about the dam came up. That's also when the first attack occurred." I didn't need to remind him that both men were also nearly bald.

He was silent for quite a while. I could just picture him stroking his silvery mustache, which he always did when he was thinking hard.

"Maybe one of them thought this would be a nice little parting gift to Cedar Hills," I said.

"Damn, Cassidy. If it is one of them, they're probably long gone by now. If they are, I'm gonna get out an APB on both of them. Haul their sorry asses in for questioning."

"It sure would help if you had some solid evidence," I said.

"I do!" he said, sounding almost cheerful. "Susie Popps, bless her soul, must've put up quite a fight. Coroner found skin under her index fingernail. Not only can we try to match blood types, but chances are the murderer also has a nice little scratch on him."

I told Booker about the hair samples I'd found in Lizzie's drain and promised to give them to Martha so she could get them to the lab. Booker admonished me to stay put, and to keep my gun close by until Martha arrived, just in case the killer came after me. I didn't tell him I'd been carrying it with me ever since I'd heard the man's voice on my answering machine. In fact, I hadn't told Booker about him calling at all. No point in getting everyone else all worried, I reasoned. But as soon as Booker hung up, I felt chillingly alone and isolated.

Chapter Fifteen

Martha came to babysit me and I made her breakfast. She looked like hell. There were dark circles under her big brown eyes and she kept eyeing my couch with obvious longing. She needed sleep.

"Here," I said, setting a plate in front of her. She had requested French toast which I made with extra-sour sourdough. I watched as she spooned on blackberry jam, lemon yogurt and powdered sugar. Martha's sweet tooth was impressive. For once in my life, I wasn't hungry, so I watched her eat while I sipped my coffee.

"If it's one of the two of them, which one would you put your money on?" she asked.

I told her about Sisson's tendency to sweat, which might explain the body odor that some of the women had reported. "And he has a handlebar moustache," I said. Martha raised one eyebrow, but continued eating. "Well, honestly, Martha. Would you trust someone with a handlebar mustache?"

"I'm trying to pretend I didn't hear that," she said, shaking her head. "Damn, these are good. Are you sure you don't want one?"

"I'm really down about Susie Popps. It hasn't even sunk in yet. I can't believe she's dead."

"Believe me. She's dead."

Sometimes I thought being a cop was starting to get to Martha. She often resorted to the kind of gallows humor that was probably only appreciated by other cops.

I was about to get us some more coffee when the phone rang. It was just the beginning of what would be a long series of calls.

"It's for you," I said. "It's Booker."

I tried to eavesdrop, but Martha wasn't saying much. When she hung up, she was frowning. "You may be right about handlebar mustaches."

"Why? What's up?"

"Well, if it is one of them, it isn't Brand. He was sacked out in his hotel room, sleeping off a serious night of drinking. Said he was at the lodge bar until two a.m. Bartender corroborates his story. So I guess we can cross him off the list."

"What about Sisson?"

"Nowhere to be found. Brand doesn't know if he stayed in town last night or not. Seems they got into a bit of a disagreement after the town meeting and went their separate ways. Booker's checking with the airport in Kings Harbor and the agency that rented him a car. He wants me to check the airports up and down the coast, as well as Portland and Eugene. It looks like it's gonna be a long day." She stifled a yawn and came over to hug me good-bye. "You sure you're going to be okay by yourself?"

I assured her I was quite safe and gave her the Tupperware container for the lab before walking her down to the dock. Looking up, I wondered how the sky could continue to be so swollen black with rain clouds without any rain actually falling.

When Martha was gone I paced the living room until I found the nerve to call Maggie. I wasn't even sure what I wanted to tell her, I just knew I wanted to hear her voice. When she didn't pick up by the fourth ring, I hung up, not wanting to leave a message. What could I say, anyway? She'd made it clear from the beginning that she wasn't interested in someone who still harbored longing for someone else. And now I'd admitted just that. Whoever said honesty was the best policy obviously had never found themselves in love with two women at the same time.

I called the women who'd spoken up at the meeting to get the details on their attacks, and added these to my charts. I spent the rest of the day racing to the phone, and by early afternoon my ear was beginning to resemble cauliflower. I carefully took notes on each call, though most weren't as helpful as I'd hoped. I divided the calls into three categories: those with information about people who did not have alibis for the dates and times in question; those who wanted updates on the status of the investigation; and those who wanted to know if I'd heard about Susie Popps. It seemed as if every woman in town considered herself my personal assistant in this case. Which in a way was nice, but I wasn't at all sure I was getting any closer to the identity of the intruder.

In between calls, I worked on my charts, attempting to sort out how many victims I actually knew about. Besides Lizzie and Sadie, there were Maggie's two clients, Gloria Baron, the two women who'd stood up at the meeting and the two callers on my answering machine. And, of course, there was Susie Popps. Assuming that none of the ones who contacted me were Maggie's two clients, and that the callers hadn't overlapped with those who'd stood up at the meeting, there were as many as ten victims. At the very least, there were six. And those were just the ones I knew about!

The sheer number of victims was beginning to say as much about "my" intruder as the crimes themselves, I thought. And he wasn't just an intruder, I reminded myself. The man I was looking for had become a killer, assuming that Susie Popps hadn't been murdered by a copy cat. I'd given enough information last night at the meeting that someone could have copied the crime fairly adeptly. Had Booker considered this, I wondered?

I was interrupted by yet another phone call and when I answered, the gravelly voice croaked, "You're next!"

I doubted it was the killer, but still, goose bumps quivered all the way down my body. I was so intent on trying to place the voice that I didn't hear the boat approach my dock. When I heard someone at the front door, I whirled around, panicked. Not only had I left my gun in the study, I hadn't locked the door.

To my relief and amazement, I saw Erica Trinidad peering at me through the sliding door, both hands cupped to the glass. When she saw me, she waved.

"I came to say good-bye," she said when I opened the door. The rain had finally started to fall and her black hair was damp.

"I'll get you a towel. Come on in."

"I knew you'd worry if I left without saying good-bye," she continued from the entryway. "And knowing you, you're probably still beating yourself up for knocking me down the other day. I came to tell you to forget it. I had it coming."

I handed her a white terry cloth towel and watched her dry herself off.

"Are you okay?" she asked, looking directly at me.

"Yeah, I'm fine. Why shouldn't I be?" I walked in through the living room to the kitchen and put some water on to boil.

"Because you look like hell."

"Where are you going?" I asked, changing the subject.

She looked almost apologetic. "Back to L.A., I guess. I can write there as well as here."

"Yeah, I'm sure you can." L.A. was where her famous movie director lived.

"Anyway, there's not much point in hanging around here."

I got out a couple of tea bags and poured boiling water into two cups, adding lemon without asking.

When I turned around, Erica was watching me with amusement.

"What?" I asked, handing her a cup.

"Oh, nothing." She headed back into the living room, sitting down on the sofa as if she owned the place.

Gammon came waddling over and plopped herself onto Erica's lap, purring shamelessly. Panic, ever jealous, leaped onto the back of the sofa and began nibbling Erica's hair while I sat alone in my favorite blue swivel chair across from them.

"What have you been feeding her?" Erica asked, shifting Gammon's considerable bulk to her other leg.

"She eats the same thing Panic does," I said a little defensively. "It's not her fault she has the metabolism of a cow."

"She's calling you a cow," Erica said to Gammon in the voice people usually reserve for infants. "But you're not a cow, are you? You're just a great big fat puddy tat." Gammon was eating up the baby-talk big time. She had even started to knead Erica's thigh. I hoped it hurt like hell. "You're not the only one who's put on weight, are you?" she continued in her singsong lilt, gingerly easing Gammon's paws off her thigh.

I was still trying not to smile when her words sank in. "What does that mean?"

"Hmmm?" Erica murmured innocently, smiling sweetly.

"Who else has put on weight?" When she shrugged, I nearly spilled my tea. "Me? You think I've put on weight?" I was incredulous.

"Well, maybe just a little."

"Really?" I stood up and felt my waist. In truth,

my jeans had been fitting perhaps a tad more snugly than before. I'd been blaming it on the dryer. "Where?" I asked, starting to panic.

"In all the right places, Cass. Trust me, it suits you."

When I caught her looking at me appreciatively, my cheeks reddened and she quickly averted her eyes. It was all I could do to not run to the mirror and check. It had never occurred to me that I might be getting fat. Erica started to laugh.

"It's not funny."

"Oh, yes, it is," she said, really getting into it.

Despite myself, I started to laugh too.

"I had no idea." She was still chuckling.

"About what?"

"That you were so vain!" she said, obviously delighted.

"I'm not," I insisted.

"You are!" She was really enjoying herself, I could see.

I sat back down, amazed that I hadn't noticed before the way the material sort of bunched up around my thighs when I sat. Damn, I thought. Martha was going to have a field day with this.

"So," she said, blessedly changing the subject. "*Have* you been?"

"Have I been what?"

"Beating yourself up for having thrown me to the ground?"

"Erica, I'm really sorry about that. I never meant to do that. It just sort of happened. If I could take it back, I would."

"That's probably what O.J. said every time he beat Nicole."

"Jesus. Is that how you see me?" It was a lousy thing to say, and she knew it.

"Of course not. That's just my way of hitting you back. Now we're even. Almost."

Feeling miserable, I sat staring into my teacup.

"You could have just said no," she said gently.

"I thought I did," I said, finally meeting her eyes. The intensity was almost more than I could bear.

"Cassidy, when I kissed you, you kissed me back."

"But I didn't want to!" I practically shouted.

"That's not how it felt."

"You felt what you wanted to feel."

"So you didn't want to kiss me?" Her blue eyes were challenging me.

"If and when I ever want to kiss you, Erica, I assure you, you will know it." This was said with much more bravado than I felt, but she'd had the upper hand far too long. Just because I'd made one terrible mistake, didn't mean I was going to put up with being bullied forever. Besides, I was really irked about the weight-gaining thing. We were saved from further torture by another phone call. I turned my back on Erica and took rapid notes as I listened.

"What was that all about?" she asked when I'd hung up.

"Just another woman not sure that her husband was home at the time of the attacks."

Erica looked at me blankly and I realized she might be the only person in Cedar Hills who was unaware of what had been happening over the past several days. Since I'd last seen her, she'd apparently been holed up at her uncle's place, working on her latest romance novel.

I took her into my study and showed her the

charts which by now covered nearly every square inch of the walls. I led her through the events as they had occurred, beginning with Lizzie's call and ending with the one I'd just had. Erica had perched herself on my desk and listened like a little kid hearing a good bedtime story for the first time. When I'd finished, it was nearly dark outside, and the rain was really coming down.

"You think it's Sisson, then?" She hopped down to examine my charts up close.

"I don't know, it's pretty weak," I said. "But he is bald, and he does sweat profusely, which might explain the body odor some women reported, and he was in Cedar Hills around the time of the first attack."

"And he's missing," Erica pointed out. "Which means you could be in danger yourself."

"Did Martha send you out here?"

"I swear to you, Cass, I didn't know a thing about any of this until right now. But if it is Sisson, he's liable to be more than slightly ticked off at you."

"That's why my gun is in here instead of hanging in the closet." I tried to sound more cavalier than I felt.

Erica was standing close enough that I could smell the hint of her perfume and I found it slightly arousing. Especially after last night's dream. I shook my head, as if that could somehow erase both the fragrance and the memories, and suddenly something that had been eluding me all day leaped out at me. I grabbed my red marker.

"What is it?"

"Last night, after my little speech to the women, Mayor Mack verbally attacked me. I was so taken aback at his calling me a dyke and being so nasty to me that the other thing I should have noticed got lost. Call it sensory overload, but I could almost swear the mayor was wearing Old Spice." In big red letters I printed Mayor Mack's name under the others I'd listed in the Old Spice column.

"What's he like?" Erica asked. The storm outside continued to pelt the windows, and the lake was getting choppy. If Erica didn't head back soon, she'd have trouble finding her way.

"He's a health freak, for one thing," I said. "Looks quite a lot like Clint Eastwood. Tries to act like him too, now that I think about it. He has a crew cut that I bet he's worn since the fifties. Probably an ex-Marine. A bit anal retentive, if you know what I mean."

"There's got to be some significance to why the intruder ties them up face down like that," she said, her quick mind already leaping ahead.

Even though she was standing right next to me, I barely heard her words. "I just thought of something else. Booker told me he couldn't find any hairs in the ski cap and I said that would make sense if the intruder was bald. But what about if he had super short hair? Like a crew cut. There's a good chance he wouldn't be able to see those hairs with the naked eye. I mean, the lab would be able to pick them up, but ..."

"You really think the mayor could be the intruder?" she asked.

It did sound absurd. On the other hand, it was interesting that last night's victim just happened to be Susie Popps, who'd publicly humiliated the mayor only hours earlier. I wondered if the other victims had had some sort of falling out with the mayor prior to their attacks. I thought of Sadie and her stand against the proposed dam two years ago. And it wasn't hard to imagine Gloria Baron challenging the mayor at one of their town council meetings. I wondered if any of the other victims had crossed swords with good old Mayor Mack. It was something I should check on right away but I'd have to be discreet.

For the first time since the investigation began, I had the feeling I might be on to something. I was anxious to run my idea by Booker. Before I could even get to the phone, it was ringing again.

"Cass? It's Rosie. I think the intruder is here!" Her voice was a strained whisper, full of panic.

"Where are you?"

"He's coming around the back. I saw him through the window. He's got a ski mask on. He's trying all the doors. I couldn't reach Tom!"

"Rosie, listen to me. Get out of the house, now. If you can, get down to the boat dock. I'm on my way. Do you have a gun?"

"He's at the back door!" she whispered. The phone went dead in my hand.

Erica had heard my end of the conversation and was already running for the dock. I grabbed my .38 and raced out behind her, my heart pumping wildly.

Chapter Sixteen

Erica's speed boat was much faster than my Sea Swirl and although it had no canvas top to protect us from the rain, Erica didn't hesitate. She started the engine, then moved aside to let me drive. I was surprised by the sheer power as I pushed the throttle forward, nearly throwing us both out of the boat. We were flying across the lake. Erica grabbed my arm and held on for dear life. I used both hands on the steering wheel and had to squint to see through the driving rain. I hoped to God Erica had put enough gas in the boat to make it all the way out to Booker's.

Neither of us said a word, nor would we have been able to hear each other had we tried. There was not another soul on the lake as we hurtled through the growing darkness toward the ranch. Damn him for living so far out, I said to myself. Hang on, Rosie, I silently chanted again and again. When at last I could make out the dimly lit outline of Booker's house, I nearly cried with relief.

A hundred feet away from the dock, I pulled back on the throttle so as not to ram it, and suddenly I saw them. Rosie had made it to the boat dock, but the man was right behind her. She was struggling to get free and he was trying to drag her back toward the house. When he saw our boat, he raised the rod in his hand and hit her over the head. Rosie fell into the water, pulling him in with her.

I could see them struggling just a few yards away but was helpless to do anything. I had my gun but didn't dare fire, afraid I'd hit Rosie by mistake. When they didn't come up, I thrust my gun toward Erica and dove in.

The lake felt warm compared to the icy rain above, but the water was black and weedy. Though it wasn't deep, I could barely make out the murky bottom ten feet below me or their struggling forms a few feet away. But what I saw was clear enough. The man was trying to drown Rosie by holding her under. With a burst of adrenaline, I launched myself through the water and grabbed him by the neck. With all my strength, I pulled him off of her, using my legs to kick at him, my fingers digging into the flesh of his thick neck beneath the sodden mask.

He turned on me then and kicked back, connecting squarely with my chin. For a brief moment, the water went totally black. But somehow I surfaced and took a giant gulp of air. Before I dove back under, I saw his massive body thrashing awkwardly through the water toward the dock. Erica was poised on the bow of the speed boat, the gun pointed right at him.

"Shoot!" I commanded, diving back under. The sound of the blast sent shock waves right through me as I fought my way through the weeds to where Rosie lay in a crumpled heap on the muddy lake floor. The second shot sounded even louder. I pulled Rosie to me, and clutched her tightly with one arm while I battled the water and weeds and struggled to the surface. When I finally reached the dock, my lungs felt as though they would burst.

Rosie's body was completely limp and weighed about a thousand pounds. It took every ounce of strength I had to push her up onto the dock. I could barely pull myself up after her. There was no time to think. I tilted her head back, pinched her nose and breathed into her mouth. Nothing. I repeated this, praying to a God I wasn't sure I believed in anymore. Still no response. I felt the carotid artery and could not find a pulse.

So I did what I remembered from eighth grade when the science teacher had brought in Annie the Dummy and made us practice CPR.

I put both hands together in an open fist and

pushed down hard beneath her sternum, hoping I wouldn't crack her ribs. I wasn't sure how many times to do this, but I knew I was supposed to alternate chest pumps with breathing. Damn, why couldn't I remember?

I called for Erica, but she was nowhere in sight. I counted out twelve chest pumps and then moved back to Rosie's side and felt her pulse. Maybe, just maybe there was a faint glimmer beneath the surface. I pushed her forehead back again, tilted her chin, pinched her nose and took a giant breath, willing life back into her as I exhaled. Nothing.

Come on Rosie, I thought, repeating the procedure. I went back to the chest-pumping, calling Erica's name as loudly as I could, but my voice was nearly drowned out by the pounding rain. My own heart was hammering uncontrollably.

At last I felt a heartbeat. I breathed into her mouth again, and finally, on the second breath, with a tremendous gush, Rosie heaved and vomited lake water all over me. It may have been the happiest moment of my life.

I rolled her over on her side and let her get the rest of the water out of her lungs. She was coughing fiercely, taking in huge gulps of air. Tears mixed with the rain running down my cheeks.

"He got away!" Erica yelled, running up to us, completely out of breath herself. "I called for an ambulance and Booker's on his way." She was leaning over, holding her sides, my gun dangling from her hand. Her chest was heaving. Rosie moaned loudly and tried to sit up. She was trembling terribly.

"Help me get Rosie up to the house!"

"I think I can make it on my own." Rosie's voice

was a harsh rasp, but it was the sweetest sound I'd ever heard.

Between us, Erica and I managed to get Rosie up the long walkway to the house, but by the time we had her inside, she was shaking violently. I helped her strip off her wet clothes, found her a bathrobe and then wrapped her in a blanket, propping her up on the sofa. Erica called to cancel the ambulance and went to the kitchen to make tea. It wasn't until the color started to return to Rosie's cheeks that Erica and I noticed we were both soaking wet ourselves.

I could hear Booker's siren growing louder as I dressed in a pair of Rosie's old sweats. She was a little bigger than I was, but sweats were sweats, I figured. They were supposed to be baggy. Erica had already changed into a faded flannel shirt and pair of worn jeans which, like everything else she ever put on, seemed to fit her perfectly. When I passed her in the hallway, I thought she looked utterly striking.

I toweled off my hair and rushed out to find Booker sitting on the couch beside Rosie, holding her hands in his. Worry etched his weathered face and his eyes were misty.

"It was one of those Ford Explorers, or Jeep Cherokees, like Cass has," Erica was telling Booker. "I couldn't tell what color it was, but if I had to guess I'd say it was dark. Definitely not white. I barely saw him through the trees though, so I can't be sure."

"Unfortunately I probably just destroyed whatever tracks he may have left with my cruiser," Booker said. "And with this rain, whatever was left is probably almost gone by now. It's coming down in torrents."

It was true. It was raining so hard outside that visibility was practically nil.

"You want me to go see if I can spot any footprints?" I asked, looking unenthusiastically out the window.

Booker chuckled. "Even if we found them, I don't have what I'd need to make a mold. And the road's so bad, I don't think anyone else is going to make it out here tonight. I nearly lost it a couple of times, getting here myself."

Rosie's voice was still hoarse but she was looking much stronger, and the color in her cheeks was encouraging. "Did you put bourbon in this?" She arched an eyebrow at Erica and held out her nearly empty cup.

Erica looked sheepish. "I thought it might help warm you up."

"Well, if you don't mind, I'd like another, with maybe just a splash more of the bourbon this time."

"Now I know she's okay," Booker said happily, taking Rosie's cup. I followed him into the kitchen.

"I don't know how to thank you." His blue eyes were wet with emotion.

"Don't." I held up my hands to stop him from going on. "It's totally unnecessary." I was afraid if I saw Booker cry, I'd really lose it. As it was, I was still feeling pretty emotional.

"There's wine in the rack," he said. His voice sounded on the verge of breaking. He turned his back to me, and I knew he didn't really want me to see him that way.

While Booker fixed Rosie's tea, I opened a bottle

of Cabernet and found two glasses. Booker popped open a can of Budweiser and followed me into the living room.

"I was aiming for his butt," Erica was saying. "I think I may have hit one of your lamp posts, though. I heard glass breaking. I wasn't even close."

Booker sat down beside Rosie on the sofa and I sat next to Erica on the loveseat. Just like Booker not to have any chairs, I thought to myself, pressing myself as far against one side as I could.

"It's not as easy as people think to hit a moving target," Booker said. "I'm just glad you two arrived when you did." He squeezed Rosie's hand and she smiled at him, acknowledging the emotion in his voice.

We let Rosie talk then, and she spoke with the stunned incredulity of someone who had just survived an airplane crash. Even so, she was a good witness. Twenty-some years of living with a cop had taught her a thing or two, I suspected.

"I'd say he was close to six feet," she said. "On the heavy side. Not fat though. But big." She went on to describe a black raincoat, the ski mask over his head, the rod in his hand. "When he saw me running down the walkway, he chased me all the way to the dock. He tried to pull me back toward the house, but when I fought back, he zapped me with that rod of his. He didn't just zap me with it though, he swung it at me hard. I ducked at the last second, or he'd have probably crushed my skull. The electric jolt would have been enough, don't you think? I don't see why he had to hit me over the head!" Rosie was

145

starting to sound a little slurry but her dark eyes had taken on a definite twinkle. She leaned forward and showed Booker the raised bump on her head.

"We should put some ice on that," he said getting up to fetch some.

"He'll be like this for days," she said, winking at Erica and me. "One time I fell off Old Red and really bruised my tailbone. Booker waited on me hand and foot. It's why I don't usually tell him when I hurt myself or am feeling poorly. He can't handle it at all."

Booker came back with an ice pack and held it gently to Rosie's head until she took it herself.

"Did either of you see anything that might help identify him?" he asked, settling back down on the couch beside her.

"He wasn't much of a swimmer," I said. "But Rosie's right. I think he must work out. He had a lot of power in his kick." I worded what I had to say next very carefully. "Did the lab ever find any hairs in the ski mask left at Susie's?"

"I told 'em it was top priority, but even so I doubt they'll get to it before tomorrow. I've been so busy trying to track down Sisson, I haven't had a chance to follow up. Why?"

"Well, it occurs to me that just because you couldn't see any hairs doesn't mean the guy is bald. If someone had very short hair, such as a crew cut, it might be difficult to see those hairs too."

"Uh huh." Booker stroked his mustache.

"So, if we knew someone who had really short hair, and who also wore Old Spice, who more or less fit the description in terms of build, would you say we might have a suspect?"

"We'd need more than that," Booker said, narrowing his eyes at me over his beer. "You got something else?"

"But then again," I went on, "it would help if he also had a motive. Something that would point to him over all others. Now, when we look at it that way, I keep asking myself, who would have a reason to be really ticked off at Susie Popps?"

"That fits with Sisson," Booker said. "After what she said at the meeting, he had to be furious with her."

"Uh huh," I said. "I wonder if anyone else might also be mad over that."

"Well, Brand, of course. But his alibi's pretty tight."

"Seems to me," Erica chimed in, knowing exactly what I was doing, "that Cassidy said Sisson was a little on the portly side. The man I saw wasn't really fat. More muscular, I'd say."

Booker was eyeing me suspiciously. "All right already. Who? Obviously you've got someone in mind."

"What kind of car does the mayor drive, Tom?"

His eyes popped open with disbelief. "You think Mack McKenzie is the intruder?" His voice had risen an octave. Rosie sat up as if to better assimilate this idea.

"I'd bet anything he was wearing Old Spice the other night," I said. "And he was so full of hatred after that meeting that he accused me of trying to turn all the women in town into man-hating dykes."

"He said that?" Rosie asked. I noticed her tea cup was almost empty again.

"Just because he was wigged out over losing the resort doesn't mean he's a killer, Cass."

"I know. But just because he's the mayor, doesn't mean he isn't."

We all sat pondering the significance of this in silence and Booker got up to freshen everyone's drinks. When he came back in he was grumbling.

"I've known Mack McKenzie for ten years now. He's one of the most popular men in town. The ladies are crazy about him. What on earth could possess a man like him to break into women's houses and tie them up? It just doesn't make any sense, Cass."

Rosie reached over and punched him in the arm. "Tom Booker, you surprise me," she said. Whenever Rosie drank, her accent grew more pronounced. "Just because Mack McKenzie is your friend doesn't mean you can ignore the facts. And just because he's popular with the ladies, doesn't mean he's not perverted. You think a man is less likely to be a weirdo if he's good looking?"

Booker stared out the window.

"It's a power thing," Erica offered, sipping her wine. "Whoever is doing this is getting off on his power over the women. And it seems to me that someone who's been mayor for ten years has already demonstrated a real taste for power. Maybe the thrill of public office just isn't enough anymore."

"And," I added, "he seems to pick especially influential women. Women who speak out or who stand up. Like he's putting them in their proper place."

"But why Rosie?" Booker asked.

It was true, I thought. Of all the women who'd been attacked by the intruder, Rosie was distinctly out of the public eye.

"Maybe because she's married to you," I said quietly. "Somebody's mad at you."

Booker's face darkened with anger, and I could tell he knew it was true. No one had any reason to pick on Rosie. The killer was sending a message to Booker.

"So," I said, not letting up on him, "just how happy was the mayor with you after the meeting?"

Booker scowled. "Somehow he got it in his thick head that I encouraged you to go to the newspaper with that story. I told him you were a big girl and didn't need my encouragement to do anything, but he was still mad. And that was before the meeting! Afterward, he wouldn't even speak to me."

"So you think it could be Mack?" Rosie asked, rubbing Booker's arm where she had hit him.

"I don't know, honey. I just don't know."

The truth was, neither did I.

Chapter Seventeen

There was no question that we'd be spending the night at Booker's. The storm continued to rage outside, and even if we'd had the Sea Swirl, I wouldn't have risked the trip across the lake. It was quite late when at last Booker announced that it was time to put Rosie to bed. She didn't put up much of a fight, although she seemed hesitant to leave us. Probably afraid of the dreams, I thought. I couldn't blame her.

"The guest room's all set up," Rosie said, lingering a little longer. "It's just a pullout, but it's pretty comfortable. I slept in there one time when Tom had the flu, and it wasn't bad at all."

"I can use the couch," I said, feeling a blush creep up my neck.

"Nonsense, Cass. This old couch isn't fit to sit on hardly, let alone try to sleep on. The pullout's a full queen-size. And there's extra blankets in the top dresser drawer."

"Come on, honey," Booker said, winking at us over her head. "Cassidy's a private investigator. I'm sure she can find the blankets."

We watched them disappear down the hallway, smiling after them. But my insides felt as if I were about to ride the world's biggest roller coaster. Too much wine, I thought, and hardly any food.

"I can sleep out here on the couch, if you prefer," Erica said, her blue eyes pinning me down. Booker had lit a fire in the fireplace, and the glowing embers played upon her skin like moonlight.

"Don't be silly," I said. "You heard Rosie. It's a big bed. I'm sure we can manage to stay on our own sides."

"You think so?" She smiled demurely. At least in the dark I wouldn't have to look at those eyes.

"Erica, you flatter yourself entirely too much. I assure you, I will somehow manage to sleep just fine. To tell you the truth, I'm exhausted." To prove this point, I yawned hugely and got up. She stayed where she was, sipping the last of the wine.

"I'll be in in a while," she said.

Fine, I thought. With any luck I'd be asleep before she got there.

I pulled the sofa bed out and quickly slipped

under the covers, leaving Rosie's sweats on. I slid as close to the wall as possible. This wasn't even my side of the bed, I thought grumpily. But I'd be damned if I'd have Erica Trinidad climbing over my body to get to her side.

Rosie may have thought the pullout was comfortable, but she clearly had more natural padding than I did. Why was it, I wondered, that there always seemed to be a spring right in the middle of where my back went? I inched over a little and curled into a fetal position facing the wall, willing myself to fall asleep.

When I heard her come in, I realized I'd been holding my breath. Oh, great, I thought. I'd have to exhale, and she'd know I was awake. As best I could, I let my breath out slowly, hoping it sounded like a gentle snore. I felt the bed sink down on her side. It seemed she was having as much trouble finding a springless place to put her body as I had. Finally she settled down and grew still.

The room was as silent as a tomb. I craved the ticking of a clock, the whirring of a ceiling fan, the blast of a furnace. But even with the steady rain outside, the bedroom was eerily quiet. And then I realized what it was. Erica was holding her breath, too. I nearly laughed aloud.

Instead, I rolled over and rearranged my body around the ghastly spring, making a lot of noise to give her the chance to exhale if she wanted. Sometimes I can be downright considerate.

But rolling over turned out to be a mistake. I could smell her damned perfume. It was the kind that smelled good in the bottle, fantastic on the skin. And on Erica, it was more than I could stand.

Despite my better judgment, I opened one eye and took a quick peek in her direction. To my dismay, she was visibly naked.

Her bare shoulder, as lovely a thing as I'd ever seen, frightened me beyond reason. Quickly, I rolled over and faced the wall once again.

I closed my eyes as tightly as I could and tried to picture something else. Wild horses running through fields of wheat. Fish swimming in a clear stream. Nothing was working. Erica's naked body was inches away.

Minutes passed, seeming longer. I heard the bedsprings creak and held my breath. There was the lightest touch, a feather brushing against my neck. I shuddered, afraid to breathe. It came again, soft but stronger, and I knew it was no accident. Erica was touching me.

My heart galloped and the moan that escaped my lips came from a place so deep I scarcely recognized it. Despite myself, ignoring every warning my brain screamed out, I turned and met her lips.

She was hot and liquid, surrounding me with her passion, enveloping me with her need. I drank her in, and felt as if I were drowning in her, hardly caring if I ever came up for air.

"So long," she murmured. "I've waited so long."

I could not answer. There were no words for what I felt.

Erica and I had never been gentle lovers. I took her hungrily, and she took me. When at last we lay spent in each other's arms, I was not surprised to feel tears on her face. There were tears on mine.

"I have always loved you," she said, nuzzling my ear. I nodded. It was all I could do.

* * * * *

The morning sun peeked through the slatted
blinds and I opened one eye, surprised to realize the
storm had passed. Not only had the rain stopped, but
the sun was shining. Erica was sprawled across my
body in a position that reminded me of what we'd
done just before finally falling asleep in the wee
hours of the morning. I tried to extricate myself
without waking her.

"Hey," she whispered, reaching out for me.

"Hey yourself." She was uncommonly pretty in
the morning light. "We really shouldn't," I said,
gently moving her hand away.

Booker's voice was suddenly audible from the
kitchen and she heaved a sigh. We dressed hurriedly,
avoiding each other's eyes, afraid of the raw emotion
between us.

"Better not look like that when we go out to the
kitchen," she warned.

"Like what?"

"Like the cat who just discovered the canary cage
has no door."

I glanced in the mirror. What I saw was a woman
who'd had very little sleep. My insides were in
complete turmoil and my mind was a jumble. What
Erica mistook for a smile was most likely chagrin. I
put on my best poker face and stumbled into the
kitchen, wondering what it was that smelled so good.
As famished as I was, I wasn't sure I could eat. My
stomach was a mess.

"Sleep okay?" Booker asked.

I could tell right away he knew. Had they heard
us? I wondered, suddenly mortified. Or was it the

look on my face? Booker had a way of raising one eyebrow that let me know he wasn't sure how he felt about it. After all, he was very fond of Maggie. I quickly shoved the thought aside and went to see what Rosie was cooking.

"*Huevos rancheros,*" she said, gently pushing me toward a chair, "and *frijoles* and tortillas and my own special salsa. Sit down."

It was a difficult meal. I was trying not to stare at Erica, who looked absolutely stunning, and Erica was trying not to look at Booker who seemed unable to look at either of us. Rosie, thank God, was either oblivious or ignoring the whole mess. She prattled on happily while I finally gave into my hunger and devoured the sumptuous breakfast.

"You never did say what kind of car the mayor drives," I said, trying to get Booker to look at me.

"Afor Robo," he mumbled intentionally, his mouth full.

"Beg your pardon?" I asked.

"I believe he said a Ford Bronco," Erica said. She had started to rub her foot across mine under the table, and I quickly pulled away. She was grinning wickedly.

"That doesn't mean he's the one," Booker said. He was definitely not in one of his best moods, I thought. "I'm still considering Sisson a suspect."

"But you're not ruling out the possibility?" I asked.

Booker finally looked right at me. "No, Cassidy. I'm not ruling out the possibility. Right after I drop Rosie off at her sister's, I'm going to look into it. I suggest you find yourself someplace safe to hide out until we catch whoever it is. If you think he attacked both Susie and Rosie because of what was said at the meeting, then it's a pretty safe bet that he's also ticked at you. Maybe you should take her out to your place." He looked pointedly at Erica. He was clearly letting us both know that he knew what we'd done, and that he wasn't particularly pleased with either of us.

"I think that's a great idea," Erica said, smiling innocently.

Booker's face reddened and he got up from the table. "I'll be outside when you're ready," he said to Rosie.

I got up and followed him. "You want to tell me why you're so upset?"

"I don't know what you're talking about." He had a toothpick in his mouth and he jammed it angrily between his teeth.

"Bull," I said. " You've been acting like a jerk all morning."

This surprised him and he turned to face me. "I just don't see you as the type to make the same mistake twice," he said. "But it's none of my business, I guess."

"No it isn't." We were standing a few feet apart, glowering at each other like tom cats.

"I thought you liked Erica," I said, feeling defensive.

"I did. But then she left for California and it didn't take a brain surgeon to see how bad you were hurting. When you got together with Maggie, I was relieved. To tell you the truth, I was beginning to think you'd die an old maid."

I laughed, and Booker did too, in spite of himself.

"So, now it's what?" he asked. "Good-bye Maggie, welcome back Erica?"

"Tom, for such a sensitive guy, sometimes you can be a real shit, you know that?"

"So Rosie tells me from time to time."

The truth was, I was more confused than I'd ever been in my life. But somehow, I didn't think Booker was going to be much help.

"She is pretty, I'll give her that," he said, stroking his mustache. "Now Maggie, she's got real class. But then, class ain't everything I guess. Did I ever tell you about Rosie's sister, Elena?"

"Why do I get the feeling you're about to?"

"Now Elena, she was a real fine girl. Hair down to her waist and the nicest set of, well, she had a real full figure. Prettiest girl in town. I wanted her in the worst kind of way. Rosie was a couple of years younger, just a skinny kid. She thought I hung the moon, of course. I'd be hanging around, waiting for Elena to notice me, and little Rosie would chat my ear off. Next thing I know, I'm lookin' as forward to talkin' to Rosie as I am to seein' Elena."

"So you ended up marrying Rosie."

"Yeah, but not before I broke her heart and made a damn fool of myself in the process." He looked at me, blue eyes challenging. "See, even when my heart knew it was Rosie I loved, and my head knew it was Rosie I loved, my damn pecker thought it was Elena. 'Course, being a girl, you ain't got that particular problem, I guess."

I wondered if Booker knew just how wrong he was.

Chapter Eighteen

Despite her insistence that I hide out at her place, I convinced Erica that I needed to talk to Lila McKenzie right away. Actually, I was glad to have an excuse to go off on my own. My emotions were a confused jumble and I wasn't ready to even think about what we'd done. Erica dropped me off at my dock and then sped away, throwing a white rooster tail behind her. I watched until her boat disappeared around the tip of the island.

By the time I'd showered and changed, it was mid-morning. I hopped into my Sea Swirl, my .38

tucked discreetly in my shoulder holster beneath my jacket, and raced across the lake for town.

The McKenzies lived just outside of town in a two-story ranch-style home built during the logging boom. It was well-cared for, with bright blue hydrangea bushes lining a brick walkway up to the front door. I was relieved to see the mayor's Bronco was not in the driveway. If it had been, I would've changed my plans in a hurry.

"Who is it?" a high, melodious voice asked through the door in answer to my knock. Evidently Mrs. McKenzie was being cautious about strangers.

"Cassidy James," I said. "Private investigator." After the meeting the other night, I knew most people probably recognized me, but I wasn't sure if the mayor's wife had even been there.

The door opened a crack, and Mrs. McKenzie peered at me through the tiny opening. "Mack's in town," she said, starting to shut the door.

"Actually, it was you I was hoping to talk to."

"Me?" She sounded as if the idea of someone actually wanting to talk to her were a foreign concept.

"It will just take a minute." I smiled harmlessly.

She considered this for what seemed an eternity and finally opened the door wide enough for me to enter. On the tall side, with an ample bosom and shapely hips, she was an attractive woman. She wore yellow slacks and a matching pullover sweater that somehow worked with her auburn hair. Her eyes were blue and well made up. Like a lot of redheads, her eyebrows and lashes would have been invisible without the aid of makeup. But despite her obvious good looks, she seemed timid and unsure of herself.

"I was just having coffee on the veranda. Would you care to join me?"

"I'd love to." I followed her through an immaculate house, full of lace doilies, miniature knickknacks and antiques. The house smelled vaguely of moth balls and I stifled a sneeze. There was not a surface that hadn't been dusted, waxed or shined to perfection, and even the kitchen looked as if it were more for show than for cooking. Mrs. McKenzie led me through French doors that opened out onto a large porch overlooking a colorful dahlia garden. The blooms were impressive. "Who's the gardener?" I asked, genuinely appreciating the rich, bright flowers.

"Oh, I am." She sounded both pleased and embarrassed. "Mack's never cared much for yardwork. That's why most of it we just let go natural. But this garden is my one little vice. I'm afraid I'm a dahlia nut." She poured coffee from a silver pot into matching china cups and sat down in a white wicker chair, motioning for me to do the same. I strangely felt as if I'd stepped onto the set for *Gone With The Wind*.

"Have you lived here long?"

"This house belonged to Mack's father. He grew up here."

"Really?" I said. "And does Tank still live here with you?"

"Oh, heavens no. Tank moved out years ago. He's got a little place in town. Well, it's not a house, really. One of those mobile homes. But it seems to suit him. Of course, he still brings his laundry by every chance he gets." She smiled indulgently, as if this were a source of pleasure for her, doing her son's laundry.

"Mrs. McKenzie," I started.

"Call me Lila, please."

"Lila," I corrected, smiling, "I guess you know the mayor's pretty mad at me for my little speech the other night. I think he feels I had something to do with people not supporting the proposed resort."

"Oh, I wouldn't know about that. Mack doesn't talk business at home."

"Were you there?" I asked. "At the meeting?"

"Why no, I wasn't. It's better I think if we keep Mack's business life separate from our home life. We learned long ago that if you bring work home with you, you may as well just stay at work. I try hard to make this home a haven, where the problems of the outside world just don't exist." She was still smiling as she spoke, looking serenely at her dahlias. I felt like I'd just entered La La Land.

"But surely you must have noticed he was upset when he got home Wednesday night?" I was trying to get her to look at me. Her eyes had such a faraway look I began to wonder if she had been dipping into the Valium jar.

"Let's see," she said, putting one lacquered red nail to her lips. "Wednesday night. Oh, yes. Mack and Tank *were* at a meeting. That's why I had supper alone. And I watched that show about sea otters. I'm sure I was sleeping by the time Mack got home. I'm not much of a night owl."

There was probably no point in mentioning that the meeting was over by eight o'clock.

"Tank works for his dad, doesn't he?" I asked, trying to figure out how I was going to broach the real subject.

"Yes. Yes, he does. He's a good boy. Mack's too

hard on him sometimes, because he doesn't have the same ambitious drive. But that's just Tank's way. He takes more after me, I guess."

"What exactly does he do?" Actually, I'd wondered this before.

"Well, he's Mack's assistant in the mayor's office, of course. And then he also helps out with the accounting business a few days a week. Mack's father left that business to Mack, and I suppose when the time comes, he'll pass it on to Tank. Why do you ask?"

Because I'm stalling, I thought.

"Well," I said, sipping my coffee. "Since you weren't at the meeting the other night, you may not know about the investigation I'm conducting."

"You mean the intruder? I read about it in the *Press*. Have you caught him yet?"

"Not yet. Actually, what I'm doing today is talking to all the women who weren't at the meeting to ask them the same questions we covered at the meeting. That way, I can rule out the men in town, one by one. Since you are the mayor's wife, I thought I'd start with you." I was hoping logic wasn't her long suit.

"Okay," she said, sounding unsure.

"Now, I'm going to ask you a lot of questions that may sound silly, or unrelated to your life, but I'd like you to answer them anyway. That way, I can say I was fair in asking all the women the same questions, without anyone receiving preferential treatment. I assure you, your answers will be kept strictly confidential." She looked at me with worried eyes and I knew I'd better start before she changed her mind. "What kind of cologne does your husband wear?"

She thought a second and then answered happily, as if she knew the answer to a difficult test question. "Old Spice," she said, smiling.

Like a teacher praising a school kid, I nodded and made a note of it. I thought what I'd do was mix in some phony questions with the real ones, like they do with lie detector tests, and watch her expressions. I prided myself on being a fairly adept lie detector myself.

"What size shoes does Mack wear?"

"Ten D," she said without hesitation.

"How old is he?"

"Fifty-one."

"Have you ever seen him wearing women's clothing?"

She laughed out loud. "Why on earth would you ask that?"

"I'm just asking everyone the same questions. Some are relevant and some aren't. It's important that you answer them all as honestly and quickly as you can. Okay?"

She looked doubtful, but nodded.

"Have you ever seen him wearing women's clothing?" I asked.

"No," she answered, still trying to suppress a smile. "Except once on Halloween a million years ago. We were just kids then."

"Do you wear pantyhose?" I asked.

"Sometimes."

"What brand?"

"Haynes."

"Does Mack ever wear pantyhose?"

"Don't be silly."

"Does he own a stun gun?"

"A what?"

"It's like a cattle prod. An electrical rod."

"Why would he want one of those?" Her brow was furrowed.

"I'll take that as a no," I said. "Do you and Mack have sex often?"

"What?"

"I'm sorry, but I have to ask. How often do you have sex?"

"Well, uh, I don't see what this has to do with anything. In fact, I don't see why you're asking me these questions at all."

"Please, Lila. Don't you see? Someone in town is bothering women. In order for me to clear Mack, or anyone else, I have to be able to rule certain things out. As soon as I can clear Mack, I can move on to the next man. It's the only way I know to be fair in this investigation."

She heaved a huge sigh and poured herself more coffee. My cup was still almost full. "Mack has always been a highly physical man," she said. "We don't make love as often as we used to, of course, but it's still a regular activity in our household."

"Thank you. Has Mack ever hit you?"

"Of course not!" she said indignantly. Her face colored at the suggestion and I knew it was time to back off.

"Does Mack like to exercise?"

"Oh yes. He works out nearly every day."

"What does he wear when working out?"

"Sweats, usually. Or shorts, depending on the weather."

"Has Mack ever demonstrated a violent temper?"

"No more than anyone else." Her gaze slid to the

left, which was what introverts did when they were lying, according to the experts.

"Has Mack ever hit you during sex?"

"Of course not!" she said. "I already told you that!"

Yeah, I thought, but just like the first time I'd asked, her cheeks turned pink at the question.

"Does Mack like Jell-O?" I asked.

Her eyes narrowed at me. "This intruder does something with Jell-O?"

It was my turn to giggle. "No," I admitted. I took another sip of my coffee. It was cold. "Does Mack have a secret place he keeps locked up, that he doesn't let anyone else get into?"

She shook her head, but she didn't seem a hundred percent sure.

"Okay," I said. "There's just one more question."

"What?" She was obviously relieved.

"Do you keep a calendar you use to write down dates and appointments?"

"Yes, why?"

"I wondered if we might look at it. There are a couple of dates I'd like to ask you about, and I thought the calendar might help jar your memory. So we can officially rule Mack out," I added.

She led me back through the kitchen to the dining room and began rummaging through a bureau drawer. Among the knickknacks, I noticed a framed photograph of the McKenzies back when Tank was only around five or six. They were all three wearing bathing suits and made a very handsome family. Mack had his arm around Lila, and both were beaming at the camera. Tank was standing in front of them, a miniature version of his father, without the grin. He was scowling with such fierce determination, it was comical. It was as close to a Norman Rockwell painting as any photo I'd seen.

"Nice picture," I said.

"What? Oh yes, it is." She gazed at the photograph fondly. "I remember when Mack took it. It was one of those self-timing cameras. He set it up himself and then ran back to where he'd left us standing. It took him about five tries to get it just right. I remember it kept going off before he could get back, or else we'd stand there waiting and waiting and then, when he'd go see what was wrong, it would go off. It was really pretty funny. As I recall, Mack was getting pretty mad at Tank and me. We were laughing like crazy."

Funny, I thought. Tank didn't look like he was laughing like crazy. Maybe Mack had just yelled at him, though, which would explain the sour expression on the kid's face.

Lila finally located the calendar and I flipped through the pages trying to get her to remember even one of the days in question, but she was next to worthless. She couldn't say for certain where Mack was on any of the days the break-ins had occurred. On two of the days she thought maybe he'd been with Tank but she wasn't a hundred percent positive. She had the memory of a gnat, I thought, but she didn't have any trouble remembering Mack taking a photograph over twenty years ago. Maybe it was just her short-term memory that was impaired.

I thanked her again for being so cooperative and let myself out the door, not sure if I'd learned anything of value or not. Lila McKenzie was a mixed bag of tricks, I thought. She was probably lying about

Mack having hit her. There was just too much blushing going on for my taste. And I'd gotten a similar reaction to the question about a violent temper. But did that make him a killer? Even I had pushed someone in anger, and fairly recently at that. That didn't mean I was a murderer. I sighed. I had no better idea about Mayor Mack than when I'd started.

Chapter Nineteen

Between Rosie's and Lila's, I'd had enough caffeine to last me a week and I needed to find a restroom. But I was anxious to talk to Tank McKenzie and see if he could clear up a few of the things his mother had so conveniently forgotten. It was after noon, but if I hurried, maybe I'd catch him before he left the office for lunch. The problem was, I didn't want to run into Mack in the process.

The mayor's office was just a block from Booker's office, and even though I'd passed it a million times, I'd never actually been inside. There was no Ford

Bronco parked in front, but even so, I was a little nervous. I cupped my hands to the window and peered in cautiously. To my relief, Tank was sitting at a desk, wolfing down a huge slice of pizza, and there was no one else in sight.

I thought about knocking, but decided against it. When I entered, Tank looked up, startled, and then smiled. "Cassidy. What a surprise," he mumbled, his mouth full of pizza.

"Is your dad in?" I asked, hoping to God he'd say no.

"Went to lunch already. You can probably catch him at the lodge."

"Oh." I hoped I sounded disappointed. "Well, maybe you can help me out." I eyed the pizza. It was pepperoni and looked delicious.

"Wanna piece?" He slid the pizza toward me. I thought about the huge breakfast I'd already eaten and the fact that Erica had said I was putting on weight. Unconsciously, I reached down and felt my waist band. Felt okay to me. I reached out and took what looked like the smallest piece, then took a dainty bite.

"I imagine your dad's pretty mad, huh?"

"I guess you could say that. But he'll get over it. He usually does."

"Has a temper, does he?"

"Yeah, I guess you could say that." Tank was beginning to repeat himself.

"Did he ever take it out on your mom?" I tried to sound nonchalant.

"Now, what makes you ask that?" He'd set his pizza down and was looking at me, his eyes challenging.

I studied Tank. He was a big man, but soft. Likeable, I thought, but not in the same caliber as his father.

"Your mom told me he hit her once. I was just curious." This was a big gamble, and I wasn't even sure where I was headed.

"She told you that?" His tone was incredulous, eyes wide.

"Uh huh." One of these days, God was going to get me for lying.

"I don't believe you." He reached over and pulled another pizza slice off, stuffing half of it into his mouth. His eyes had shut down and I knew he was holding something back.

"Tank." I reached out and touched his hand but he pulled it back as if my fingers were fire.

"That wasn't all she told me," I said. "I know about the other, too. But I'd like to hear it from you."

My heart was in my throat. I had no idea what I was searching for, only that I sensed there was something there. Tank put his pizza down and when he looked at me, his eyes were wet and shiny.

"My mother doesn't have the good sense to know when to keep her mouth shut, does she?"

"It helps sometimes to talk about these things. I think it helped her, anyway." I was reaching so far I was afraid I'd fall flat on my face, but Tank seemed lost in his own thoughts. He let out a gargantuan sigh.

"I suppose if you know, it doesn't really matter." His shoulders heaved and he sat back in the chair, looking for all the world like a beaten dog.

"I was very young," he said. "Did she tell you

how young I was? And it was raining. I remember that very clearly. I'd been in bed because I had a cold. I remember that too. Isn't that funny? To remember something as insignificant as a cold?"

"Go on," I said.

"I heard noises. At first I thought it was a bad dream. Then I realized the sound was coming from my parents' bedroom. My mommy was screaming. I was only six, you understand. But it was my mommy and she was being hurt." His shoulders sagged, and his hand came up to his brow, visibly trembling.

"It was your father?"

He looked at me as if I'd stolen his punch line. His eyes narrowed, and then he did something that disturbed me. He laughed. "Yes. It was my father. The mayor. Does that shock you? Of course, he wasn't mayor back then."

"What happened?"

"Well, as I said, I was only six. But that didn't stop me from trying. You see, I rushed into my parents' bedroom to help my mother and what do you think I found?"

I realized he was challenging me. We'd both put our pizzas down and our hands were on the table inches apart.

"He was beating her?"

"Oh, yes," he said, his voice strained. "Apparently she had refused to engage in his version of an afternoon delight. Of course, I didn't know anything then. Only that he was hurting her. She saw me first, you know."

"What did she do?"

"Well, he was on top of her, you see, from behind. When she turned her head and saw me, she shook her head, telling me to go. But she was crying and, well, I couldn't just leave her there. I went after him. I'd like to think I was being brave, but it was pure instinct." Tank's voice was about to break, and he held his hand to his mouth to ward off the sobs just beneath the surface.

"He was raping her?" I could tell this was causing him great pain, but I didn't know how else to do this. He nodded, trying to check his emotions. "What happened next?"

"Well, I guess it was a good thing I got there when I did. You know, maybe he was embarrassed or something. Anyway, he stopped what he was doing, and that was that."

"You mean he just stopped?"

He nodded, his head bobbing as if he were the six-year-old he was remembering.

"And after that?" I asked.

"What do you mean?"

"I mean, did it ever happen again?"

"Oh, no. That was it. Of course, I understand now, that in those days he was drinking. He's never touched another drop since. At least not since I've been old enough to remember. But I'm pretty sure the whole thing was on account of him drinking too much at the time. I guess some men get that way."

"What did your mother do?" I asked, gently. "I mean, after you stopped him?"

He looked baffled at the question.

"I mean, did she talk to you about it? Did she lock him out of the house? Did she yell and scream?"

"No, no, no," he was saying, shaking his head. "Obviously, you don't know my mother. She would never talk about something like that. Unpleasant things just don't exist for Lila McKenzie. She just pretended it never happened."

"How about your dad? Did he ever talk to you about what happened?"

"Not that I recall. I really don't remember much except what I told you. I'm surprised I remember that much. Most of my childhood is a blur."

"Well, that was a pretty traumatic event for a six-year-old kid to witness. I'm not surprised you remember it so well. But you get along with your dad okay now, it seems like."

"Oh, sure. Sometimes he's a bit overbearing, you know. But deep down he's a good man. He's not your intruder, Cass, if that's what you're trying to get at."

"What makes you say that?"

"Come on, Cassidy. I'm not stupid. Why else would you be talking to my mom about whether my father has ever beaten her? Obviously the intruder must beat his victims. But just because he hit her and forced her to have sex with him that one time a million years ago doesn't mean he's a bad man. Everyone should be entitled to one mistake in a lifetime."

I wasn't sure I'd consider beating and raping your wife a mere mistake, but I wasn't about to argue the point with Tank. He was obviously still traumatized by the childhood event.

"To tell the truth, Tank, I'm asking everyone the same questions. But one thing that does bother me is that your mother couldn't vouch for your father's whereabouts on any of the dates in question. She said maybe you could help."

Tank gave a short, derisive laugh, and reached for his pizza. "My mother couldn't vouch for her own whereabouts on any given day. As I'm sure you noticed, she doesn't always have both oars in the water."

"I found her a sweet, pleasant woman. She obviously cares a great deal for you."

"Oh, sure," he said. "I didn't mean to sound critical. It's just the way she is. I accepted it a long time ago. Of course, she wasn't always like that. There was a time when she was younger that she was quite the lady about town. PTA president, that kind of thing. But over the years, she's just sort of slipped away."

"So, can you?" I asked, feeling like a total heel for bringing so much old pain to the surface. Tank looked at me blankly. "Can you vouch for your father's whereabouts on the days in question?"

"Believe it or not, I already checked. Not that I was thinking that he had anything to do with it, you understand. It's just that when you had us all write down the dates, I went back to see what I was doing at those times. You'd be surprised how hard it is to remember stuff like that. But I was able to figure it out for the most part. Not that it's going to help much." He let out a short chuckle and shook his head.

"What do you mean?"

"On two of the dates I was covering for my dad." When I looked at him blankly, he smiled sadly and said, "You see, I was already serving as my father's alibi."

I raised my eyebrows. I had no idea what he was talking about.

"He cheats on her," he finally blurted. "But he doesn't want to hurt her. Quite often he uses me as his alibi. 'Tank and I are going to go to dinner in Kings Harbor.' 'Tank wants me to go bowling with him tonight.' Like that. He always tells me what he's told her, in case she asks. The funny thing is, she hardly ever does."

"So your dad was seeing someone on the dates in question?"

"Two of them for sure. I'm not positive about the other. Obviously I don't remember the one two years ago. But the two most recent ones, yeah."

"Do you mind my asking who he was seeing?" My heart was pounding a little erratically. This was going better than I could have ever dreamed.

"I have no idea," he said. "And that's the truth. Even if I did know, I probably wouldn't tell you. I mean, I assume it's someone in town. Probably married. Trust me, there's no shortage of women willing and ready. He seems to attract them like flies."

"Well, the problem is, Tank, that that leaves your father without any alibis at all on the dates in question."

"You're barking up the wrong tree," he said, starting to look angry. "Just because my dad said what he did the other night doesn't mean you have the right to accuse him of being a murderer. He's the mayor, for God's sake. You could hurt his reputation just by asking these questions. I suggest you go find someone else to harass."

He stood up and leaned toward me, hovering over the pizza between us. Out of practice, I sniffed, though I didn't expect Tank to be wearing Old Spice. He wasn't. And he also wasn't wearing much deodorant, I thought, wondering why so many men in Cedar Hills seemed to like the smell of their own sweat. Maybe it was a macho thing women just didn't understand. Whatever it was, the smell didn't go too well with pepperoni pizza.

"Tank, I appreciate your taking the time to talk to me. I really do. And I didn't really mean to sound accusatory toward your dad. I'm just trying to clear people one by one, so I can cross them off the list." I tried to flash him my best Miss Innocent smile, but I'm not sure it came off just right. As I headed for the door, he called after me.

"A word to the wise. You may want to hold off on questioning him today, Cass. I'm afraid you're not among his favorite people right now. Give him a chance to cool down over this resort thing, and maybe you'll stand a better chance of getting him to talk."

"Thanks, Tank. I appreciate the advice. And thanks for the pizza, too."

I let myself out, my head swimming as badly as my bladder. If I didn't find a restroom fast, I thought, hightailing it to Lizzie's tavern, I was going to embarrass myself.

Chapter Twenty

After I'd used the facilities, I let Lizzie buy me a beer. It was Friday and the place was already packed with lunchtime drinkers. I realized as soon as I sat down that I wasn't going to be able to hear myself think, which was what I really needed to do. But after that pizza, I was pretty thirsty, and one beer shouldn't impair my cognitive skills too much, I told myself.

"You caught that pre-vert yet?" Gus Townsend asked.

"I hear tell he's the same one that kilt little

Susie Popps. Looks like he ain't just a perv no more," Ed Green chimed in.

Within minutes, the entire bar was into the conversation. I shrugged at Lizzie and gulped my beer as fast as I decently could. Even so, it was difficult to pry myself loose from the questions long enough to make my escape.

"See you around, Cass," Lizzie called as I edged my way out the bar.

Susie's death had shaken everyone in town, but none more than the intruder's previous victims. They knew it could just as easily have been them. But instead of fear, I saw fierce determination in Lizzie's eyes. In fact, she was starting to look like her old self. After last night's public statement to the other women she seemed to have regained a bit of the bounce in her step.

I wasn't sure what my next move ought to be. I needed to talk to Booker, but when I walked past the sheriff's office it was still closed. He was probably still out looking for Sisson, I thought. I passed the mayor's office, thinking I would just walk around for a while to sort out my thoughts. I noticed Tank was no longer inside and the Closed sign was propped up in the window. I was about half a block away when an idea popped into my head, and before I could talk myself out of it, I wheeled back around and headed straight for the mayor's office.

Like the sheriff's office, the mayor's was an old two-bedroom house that had been converted to accommodate a business. Which meant there was probably a back door, I thought. I looked to make sure no one could see me, then edged around the side of the building. The door was locked.

Why was it, I wondered, that I never had my lock picks with me when I needed them. Because, Cassidy, I chided myself, you didn't know that you'd be breaking and entering when you left the house.

I sidled around the perimeter, checking windows, but those, too, seemed securely locked. Without my picks, I was going to have to rely on an old burglar's trick. I couldn't just kick in the door — I was afraid the noise might alert someone. I returned to the back door, removed a credit card from my wallet and worked it between the jamb and lock. Somewhere, a dog barked, causing me to jump. I slid the plastic card back and forth until finally, the metal lock clicked and the door swung open on its hinges.

I quickly slipped inside and closed the door behind me, my heart pounding in my chest. If the mayor or Tank returned now, I'd be in deep trouble. I could lose my license for what I was doing.

Like a cat burglar, I padded into what had once been a bedroom but now served as the mayor's private office. I didn't know exactly what I was looking for, but I opened drawers, peeked in closets, looked behind books on the bookshelf, hoping I'd find something that would point to the mayor's guilt. The only thing remotely interesting was a package of Twinkies hidden beneath a manila file folder. Apparently Mr. Health Nut was a closet junk-food nibbler. For some reason this cheered me a great deal.

I moved into the next room, which was much smaller and not nearly as neat. This must be where Tank did whatever it was he did as the mayor's assistant. I gave it the same attention I'd given the other room, with the same dismal results. I checked my watch and was surprised to see how much time had passed. I was pushing my luck and I knew it, but snooping is an addictive vice. I just couldn't leave the job unfinished.

I checked the tiny bathroom next, looking in the toilet tank and under the bath mat, not really expecting to find anything, but checking just the same. I found nothing.

It was in the kitchen that I finally stumbled upon something, quite literally. The floorboards of the house were all original hardwood, with small throw rugs scattered about for color. The rug in the tiny kitchen was bunched up, causing me to trip. Which in turn caused me to look beneath it, thinking how frequently people used rugs to hide floor safes. I immediately checked all of the other throw rugs in the house and was disappointed when no floor safe was discovered. But the idea of a safe was firmly planted in my mind and I went back into the mayor's office determined to find one, if it existed.

It was so obvious, it nearly leaped out at me. The mayor had decorated the walls of his office with the kind of pictures and bric-a-brac that only hunters could appreciate. Western scenes of cattle drives and antlered deer heads mounted on plaques just don't turn me on. But behind the head of a giant buck I finally found what I had been looking for.

The safe was less than a foot in diameter and looked hand-crafted. Someone had chiseled a hole in the wall, framed it with wood and inserted a metal box, over which another wooden frame was hammered. It wasn't fancy, but it served its purpose. Even better, the keyhole in the small spring door looked relatively unsophisticated and simple to pick.

Once again, I could have kicked myself for not having brought my picks. Well, I'd just have to improvise.

I poked around in the mayor's desk selecting items that might work. I took a paper clip, a pair of scissors which looked too big, and some fingernail clippers. After ten minutes, I put them all back, discouraged. It was really getting late, and I knew I was pushing it, but I was so close! I felt sure that if the mayor were the killer, he'd need a place to hide the knife he'd used to kill Susie. Unless he'd already discarded it. But even if he had, I was sure that somewhere he still had the stun gun and the nylons. And what better place than the safe in his office?

I should, of course, have waited for Booker to get a warrant and done it the legal way. But without real evidence, there was no justification for a warrant. And anyway, my impatience was getting the better of me.

It was in the kitchen that I found what ended up working, the short prong of an Ahso wine opener. What the tee-totaling mayor needed a corkscrew for was beyond me — but I was thrilled he had it. Maybe he allowed his visitors to imbibe. With just a few minor adjustments, I was finally able to spring the metal lock.

My heart was pounding so hard when I opened the safe that I didn't hear the front door open until it was too late. When I did hear it, I stood, petrified, in front of the open safe, staring with open mouth at the rows of plastic L'eggs containers beside what was undoubtedly a stun gun and a wicked-looking hunting knife. Two black woolen ski masks sat behind it all, the price tag still attached to one. I quickly shut the safe and hefted the gruesome deer head back onto the wall. My hands were shaking as I headed for the back door, hoping whoever had just entered was still out in the front room. But when I turned the corner, I came face to face with Mayor Mack in the hallway.

"What the hell?" he said, jumping back. His face quickly went from surprise to anger. "Do you mind telling me what you're doing in my office?" It really wasn't a request. The blue vein beneath the skin on his neck was already pulsing away.

"Looking for you, actually," I said, trying to sound calm. My heart was racing.

"I'm calling the police right now," he said, stepping toward me.

"Good. I was about to do that myself."

"What's that supposed to mean?"

"I think you have a pretty good idea what I'm talking about, Mack. But go ahead." I was standing just outside the doorway of his office and there was no way I could slip past him to make a run for the back door. I was in a sticky situation. At the moment, he didn't know I'd found the evidence. If I could just bluff him long enough to get myself out and find Booker, maybe I'd have a chance. On the other hand, that might give him time to get rid of the evidence.

He took the decision out of my hands by stepping around me into his office. I turned to watch him, and saw with dismay that the deer head was hanging at an awkward angle. It didn't take Mack long to see it too. He looked back at me, eyes wild with rage.

"I'm placing you under citizen's arrest," I said, pulling out my .38.

His eyes had become tiny slits in his crimson face. "And I'm charging you with breaking and entering!" he shouted. "You have no right to invade the sanctity of this office!"

"Put your hands up, Mayor. Please."

"Or what? You going to shoot me? Go ahead, I dare you."

Geez, now he even *sounded* like Clint Eastwood. If I hadn't been so terrified, I might have found it funny.

Mayor Mack walked slowly toward me, and I could have kicked myself for the way my hand was trembling. He saw it too, and snickered.

"That's far enough," I said. He was only a few feet away and I could see the blue vein throbbing erratically. My hand tightened on the gun, my finger firm against the trigger.

"What's going on?" The voice came from behind me.

I whirled around, and when I did, Mack leaped at me, catching my hand in both of his and twisting until the gun fell harmlessly to the floor.

"Tank, get the sheriff!" I yelled, twisting with the pain that shot through my wrist.

"Stay where you are!" the mayor barked.

"Would someone please tell me what's going on?"

"This bitch just broke into my office is what's going on," the mayor said. He still had my wrist twisted back, and I had broken out in a cold sweat from the pain.

"Tank, just get Booker for me. You've got to trust me on this!" I pleaded. His eyes were wild, darting from his father to me and back again. But his feet seemed rooted to the ground.

"Just go back home, son. I'll take care of this. No need for you to get involved. Go on, now."

My eyes had started to water, but I was helpless to do anything about the position I was in. If I moved, I knew my wrist would snap.

"Look in the safe, Tank!" I said. When he looked at me blankly, I pointed my chin toward the wall. "Behind the deer head. Just open it!"

Tank stood for what seemed an eternity, deciding. Finally, he shrugged and walked toward the mounted deer head. He had to skirt the two of us, and when he did, he reached down and retrieved my gun which had skittered across the floor. He turned and aimed it at me.

"I got her now, Dad. You can let her go. It looks like you're kind of hurting her."

To my intense relief, Mack let go of my hand. We stood, inches apart, looking expectantly at Tank. I tried to ignore the pain shooting up to my shoulder.

"What now?" Tank asked.

Mack held his hand out for the gun and stepped toward his son.

"Wait!" I shouted. "Look!" I rushed toward the safe and before the mayor could stop me, I hefted the mounted deer head and flung it to the floor. The safe door was still slightly ajar and I pulled it open.

"There! Don't you see?"

Tank was standing slack-jawed, staring into the safe. The mayor's face had turned a mottled purple. Slowly, as if under water, Tank turned the gun so that it was pointed toward his father, then swung it back toward me.

"The person who killed Susie Popps used a knife like this, Tank. The man who broke into all those women's homes wore a ski mask just like these, only he left his at Susie's so he had to buy a new one. Look, Tank, the price tag is still on one. And he used nylons to tie them up with. He used a stun gun to make them unconscious, Tank. I'm sorry, but it's true!"

"She planted all that! Tank, you've got to believe me! She broke in here and planted this evidence! You can't possibly believe what she's saying!" Mack's voice had the ring of hysteria.

Tank moved backwards toward his father's desk and picked up the telephone. His right hand still held my gun which was now trained solely on his father. His left hand punched numbers and I held my breath. "Rita? This is Tank. Listen, is the sheriff in? Would you ask him to run over here right now? We've got a bit of a situation over here. Uh, yeah, I guess you could say it's an emergency. I just found out that my father killed Susie Popps."

Tank barely had time to put down the receiver before his father rushed him. He moved like a wild animal, raw muscle fueled by rage. I did not want to see Tank shoot his father. With pure instinct, I grabbed the hideous deer head and with one hand swung it at the mayor's head as he dove for his son. The two heads collided and the mayor fell limply to the ground.

My gun still clutched in his trembling hand, a mixture of shock and dismay on his whitened face, Tank was standing over the inert body of his father when Booker rushed in.

Chapter Twenty-one

Sadie Long had outdone herself, I thought, marveling at the speed with which she'd put out the special edition of the *Cedar Hills Press*. Obviously she'd been up all night so it would be ready for Saturday morning. It was four pages total and completely dedicated to the Masked Intruder, as everyone had taken to calling him.

There was even a picture of me on the front page, talking at the meeting. There were interviews with some of the women who'd been attacked and a lovely piece on Susie Popps, with speculation that the brave speech which saved the town from the proposed resort had also led to her untimely death. The entire back page was dedicated to the life and times of Mack McKenzie, including pictures of him as a small, smiling boy growing up in Cedar Hills; another of him in high school after winning the annual Island Swim Tournament, a giant trophy held aloft; a later picture of him wearing a white sailor uniform, his arm around Lila; and finally one of him addressing the meeting on Wednesday night. Sadie had snapped him right after Susie's speech and captured the wild rage in his eyes perfectly. Seeing that picture, no one would have trouble believing the mayor was capable of the crimes that had been committed.

It was only noon, but Lizzie's tavern was standing-room only. I had a stool next to Booker and Jess and had not been able to buy myself a beer. As it was, I had three sitting in front of me. Everyone, it seemed, wanted to buy me a drink. It wasn't unusual for people to be drinking at noon on a Saturday in Cedar Hills, but it was unusual to have so many women in the bar. There was a touch of festivity, despite everyone's shock that Mayor Mack turned out to be the intruder. Everyone was talking at once and poor Lizzie was being run ragged. I thought she looked at least ten years younger than a week ago. She was actually smiling.

"That wasn't the only stuff we found in that safe, by the way," Booker was saying. "He also had some damned incriminating papers signed by him, Sisson and Brand. Seems Mack was due some pretty hefty kick-backs if the resort had gone through."

"No wonder he was so hot to trot on that thing," Jess said.

"I never did trust a man who wouldn't drink a beer now and then," Gus Townsend volunteered.

"Yeah, well, you can bet Brand and Sisson won't be showing their faces around here any time soon. That whole deal was shady as hell. No wonder Sisson high-tailed it outta here so fast after that meeting. He must've known the whole thing was about to blow."

"I just feel sorry for Tank," Tommy Greene said.

So did I, I thought, wondering where Tank was now. Which made me think again about Lila McKenzie. Booker had broken the news to her last night, and he said she'd reacted strangely. "Didn't even break down and cry," Booker had said. Apparently the ozone layer was pretty thick around La La Land. Hard to break through.

"The one I feel for is Susie Popps," someone said. This sobered everyone, and people reached for their glasses. Jess helped himself to one of mine.

"How'd you get them articles all typed up so fast, anyways?" Tommy asked Sadie. Sadie was drinking straight whiskey, and every time she downed one, Lizzie gave her a refill. The two of them seemed to be hitting it off pretty well.

"I was going to do a special on the intruder any-way. Then when Susie died, I wrote an article on her. It all just kind of fell together. It's amazing what you can accomplish with computers these days." She winked across the bar in my direction.

Yeah, I thought, and when you've been bottling something up inside for so long. Like Lizzie, Sadie looked a younger, more vibrant version of her former self. Even her cheeks glowed.

Erica was sitting on the other side of Sadie,

sipping a glass of red wine. Lizzie's wine selection was limited to your basic colors; white, pink and red. It was probably better not to ask the label. Erica was taking little sips and trying valiantly not to wrinkle her nose.

"Is the mayor still claiming that Cassidy framed him?" she asked Booker. It was the first time they'd spoken since the other morning, and I was relieved to see Booker smile at her. I'd barely had time to talk to her myself, things had been happening so fast since the mayor's arrest.

"Whining like a stuck pig. Got himself a lawyer from Kings Harbor, but I don't think even she believes him. Don't tell anyone I said that. I'm sure they'll ask for a change of venue for the trial. He doesn't stand a prayer around here."

"His best chance for living is if he stays in jail, far as I'm concerned," Lizzie said. Sadie beamed at her with big, glistening eyes.

"I wish they'd let him out, just for one night. That's what I wish," Julie Jones said. She'd worked with Susie in the real estate office and was taking the loss hard.

"Where's Rosie?" I asked Booker.

"Oh, she didn't feel like coming down. Said she wanted to do some baking today. She puts me on these damn diets and then gets in one of her baking moods. I tell you, Cass, it's hard work being married to a good cook."

Erica had started giving me the eye, and I wasn't sure what I was going to do about it. Things had happened so fast I'd scarcely had time to work things out in my own mind. I needed time to think, and the tavern wasn't the place to do it. I'd really only come in because Jess insisted that I meet them all for a drink and because I'd wanted to see Sadie's special edition. Now that I had, there was one last thing I wanted to do before heading back, and I was dreading it. I excused myself from the crowded bar and stepped out into the blinding daylight, Erica right behind me.

"Why do you feel you need to go?" she asked. We were walking north, toward the outskirts of town, instead of back toward the marina.

"It's just something I think is the right thing to do. Call it a Random Act Of Kindness," I said. When she looked at me questioningly, I explained Tommy's newest crusade, and we both laughed. But by the time we got to the McKenzies' driveway, I was beginning to kick myself for having come. My stomach was in knots. There was no answer to my knock, and the doorbell didn't work. I tried the door, but it was locked. "Come on," I said. "Let's go around back."

Lila was where I figured she'd be, tending her dahlia garden. She was wearing a pretty yellow shirt tucked into a pair of old jeans and her face was made up perfectly. She had on pink garden gloves and a giant straw hat to protect her fair skin from the sun. She was bent over, studiously pulling weeds from the garden.

"Lila?" I asked tentatively. I didn't want to startle her.

When she looked up, I could see the faraway look that had bothered me yesterday. If anything, she looked even more distant than before.

"I came to see if you were okay, if you needed anything."

She went back to her digging, shaking her head.

"I'm sorry about what happened," I said. I wondered if she knew the details. I wondered if she'd talked to Tank. "Lila." My voice seemed to startle her. She stood up.

"Are you going to be all right?"

She looked at me as if I had asked her to recite Homer's *Odyssey*. Then her eyes cleared a bit, and one small tear slid silently down her cheek.

"Why don't we go up on the veranda?" I said. She nodded, and led the way. Erica, who'd kept her distance, followed behind.

"Did you know they think Mack is a killer?" she said to me, her eyes wide with wonder. "Can you imagine such a thing?" She sat down in the white wicker chair and looked straight at me.

"Do you remember yesterday when I asked you if Mack had ever hit you?" She nodded, biting her lip. "You didn't tell me the truth, Lila. Why not?"

Another tear rolled down her cheek, but she seemed oblivious to it. "I try not to remember," she said, looking helpless.

"It's important that you do remember, Lila. It will help you get through this whole mess. You do remember, don't you?"

She shook her head, denying it, but as more tears fell, her head began to nod instead.

"Go ahead, Lila. It will help to talk about it." I wasn't sure why I was doing this, but Lila McKenzie needed a friend.

"It was so long ago," she said. "Mack was different in those days. He was drinking a lot and he was angry a lot. He came home early one day and found me sitting talking to the milkman. We still had milkmen back then. It was completely innocent. We often sat and had a cup of coffee together. But Mack didn't believe me. He went wild. He wanted to have sex right then." She paused, embarrassed. "I told him it was my time of the month, but he didn't care. Said he was my husband and I'd by God do what he wanted when he wanted. He was scaring me, he was so angry." Her eyes were glazed over again and she was reciting the story as if it had happened to someone else. "He forced me into our bedroom and I told him again that I didn't want to, and he . . . that's when he hit me." She looked up at me, as if that were the end of the story.

"And then?" I asked.

"Oh, well. We did. Have sex, I mean."

"What kind of sex, Lila?"

Her eyes grew wide at the question.

"He raped you, didn't he? It wasn't sex, it was rape. He forced you, Lila. That's not sex, that's rape."

This time her eyes squeezed shut, and more tears slid out the corners of her eyes. She was nodding.

"And then Tank rushed in."

"How do you know all this?" she wailed. "I've never told anyone!"

"Tell me what happened, Lila."

"Poor little Tankie," she said, her voice trembling. "He was so pathetic. Trying to protect me from his own father. I tried to tell him to go away, but he wouldn't listen. Finally Mack picked him up and took him away."

"Took him where?" I asked. Tank hadn't told me this.

"Back to his room!" she cried. Her shoulders had started to heave, and she was having trouble getting the words out. "He was yelling and screaming, calling 'Mommy, Mommy, Mommy,' over and over again, but I was just so mortified, so humiliated, and I thought Mack was just spanking him, you know, and that it would be over soon. And then it was." She paused to catch her breath. "I was so relieved it was over. I kept waiting for Mack to come back into the bedroom, but he never did. He left the house and didn't return that night. I was just too mortified to face Tankie. When he didn't come out of his room that night, I thought he was probably as embarrassed as I was. It was an awful feeling. It wasn't until the next day that I realized what Mack had done. How he had beaten Tank with his own little belt, over and over. When I found Tank still tied up like that, with his underwear stuffed into his mouth, I was so angry! The poor boy had a terrible cold, and there he was shivering naked on the hard wood floor, barely able to breathe'"

My stomach had bunched itself up in knots, and I felt queasy.

"You, er, Mack left him like that all night?" I asked, barely able to get the words out. "What did you do?" I didn't mean it to sound so accusatory, but I couldn't help it.

"Nothing." She was sobbing. "I didn't do anything. I pretended like it never happened! He didn't do it very often, you see. Only when he drank. And he never hit me again after that first time." She took a deep breath, and I noticed her nose had started to run, but she seemed oblivious to this detail. "Poor, poor Tankie," she went on. "He tried so hard to please his father, was so afraid to make a mistake. But there was always something — a broken vase, a messy room. You just never knew what would set Mack off." Her intermittent sobbing made it difficult to hear her words. "I learned not to interfere. It was best just to let him get it out of his system, you see. After that first time, he always left Tank tied loosely enough that he could eventually get himself free. And then it would be over and everything would be back to normal for a while."

The enormity of what she was saying was beginning to sink in. And suddenly, I thought I might be sick.

"Let me see the paper," I said to Erica, who'd brought the special edition in her purse. I turned to the back page and stared at the picture of a young Mack McKenzie hefting a huge trophy high above his head. He was wearing swim briefs and a triumphant smile. "Mack must have been quite a swimmer," I said to Lila.

"Yes, yes he was. He still loves to swim."

"And Tank?" I asked, dreading the answer.

"Hates the water," she said. "His dad threw him in the lake when he was only four, saying it was the best way to teach a kid to swim, but it didn't work. He nearly drowned, poor Tank. Cried for hours. Even as an adult, he never liked to go for boat rides. Still can't swim very well, as far as I know."

And neither could the man who tried to kill Rosie, I thought, remembering the awkward thrashing of Rosie's attacker. Those were not the graceful moves of a former swim champ. They were the desperate moves of a man afraid of the water.

Erica's eyes had grown huge and I knew she was thinking the same thing I was. "If Tank saw this paper," she started.

"Then he knows we know." We were already on our feet. "Lila, listen to me. Lock the doors and don't open them for anyone. Not even Tank."

"But why?" she asked, looking scared. "I don't understand!"

But I did. I had just nailed the wrong man. And the real killer had helped me do it, after framing his own father. And he'd almost gotten away with it, I thought, running for the door. But there were three of us who knew the killer couldn't swim. Starting with Rosie.

Chapter Twenty-two

Erica and I ran full speed back toward town. She ducked into Lizzie's tavern to get Booker, while I raced ahead to the marina. I didn't know which one of us would get there first, but at least we'd have both exits covered. I just hoped we weren't too late. I was relieved beyond belief that I'd left my .38 in the boat the night before.

I roared through the channel, breaking all speed limits, and raced across the lake toward Booker's, wishing I were in Erica's speed boat instead of the Sea Swirl. I pushed it full throttle, willing the boat to go faster. It seemed to take an eternity to get there.

The house looked the same as always, and I began to think that perhaps I'd overreacted. Maybe I was wrong about Tank. But I didn't think so. At any rate, I could hardly take that chance.

I raced up the long walkway to the house, listening for sounds of danger. The only thing I heard was the soft nickering of the mustang when I passed her corral. Apparently, I'd beaten Erica and Booker to the ranch.

I stepped up onto the back porch, my gun drawn, feeling silly. If Rosie weren't in any danger and she stepped out onto the porch, she'd probably have a heart attack, I thought. I peered through the back-door window, cupping my hands to the glass.

At first I thought it was just Rosie, peering into the oven. When you see something you've heard about, but never actually seen before, it sometimes takes the mind a moment to assimilate the data. When I realized what I was really seeing, I burst through the door, my heart thundering.

Tank looked up, surprised, still holding Rosie's squirming body beneath him. I could not see Rosie's head. It was in the oven.

"Let her go, Tank," I said, my gun aimed right between his eyes.

"You shouldn't have come, Cass. I was hoping you wouldn't." He seemed genuinely sad to see me. Still, he held Rosie's head in the oven. I could smell the gas from across the room.

I tightened my grip on the gun and stepped toward him. "Let her go, now!"

"I have to do this, don't you see? I never meant

to hurt anyone, not really. And then you started in and Susie saw my face and everything just happened. I've got to fix it now, before it all falls apart."

"It's too late for that, Tank. Let her up."

"Not if I make it look like she killed herself. Distraught over what almost happened to her, or something. Otherwise, I'd have to spend my whole life worrying about when she, or you, or your girlfriend would figure out that it couldn't have been my dad who tried to kill her. If it hadn't been for that stupid picture in the paper, of him winning that ridiculous swim trophy, none of this would have had to happen."

Rosie was kicking violently, trying to get herself free, and Tank was having a difficult time positioning her head and talking at the same time. He was out of breath.

"You going to stick my head in the oven too, Tank?" I asked. Rosie had started to cough uncontrollably, and if I didn't get her out soon, I feared she would asphyxiate.

"I was thinking about an accidental fire. I didn't want to have to kill you, Cass. I actually liked you. And you were so easy to manipulate."

I didn't like the way he was referring to me in the past tense. "I'm warning you, Tank. If you don't let go of her on the count of three, I'll shoot." I counted aloud. He didn't budge.

I didn't know if I could do it. My hands trembled and the gun felt slippery in my palm. But Rosie had quit resisting and her body was starting to go slack. I held the gun with both hands and pulled the trigger.

Tank screamed and rolled across the kitchen floor,

holding his shoulder. Rosie fell to the floor, coughing and gasping for air. I rushed to where she lay and helped her to her feet. I turned off the gas, starting to cough myself, and threw open the window.

"Are you all right?" I asked. Her eyes were huge, with tears streaming down her face. But she nodded, struggling for breath. "Go wait in front. Booker's on his way. Get as much air into your lungs as you can!"

When I turned back, Tank was already out the back door, running toward the lake. I raced after him.

I could tell he was hurting by the way he held his arm when he ran, but it didn't seem to slow him down much. I'm a pretty fast runner, but I was having trouble keeping up with him.

I rounded the bend in the walkway and realized I'd lost sight of him. He wasn't on the dock. Where else could he have gone? And then I heard a familiar whinny and knew exactly where he'd gone. Tank was with the horses.

"Come on out, Tank. You can't hide forever. Give yourself up!"

I was edging toward the stalls, searching for a movement that would give away his position. There were too many places to hide. I held my gun in both hands, straight out in front of me, trying to ignore the pounding of my heart as I inched forward. Suddenly, I heard a loud crack and wheeled around to see Tank barreling straight toward me, astride the Appaloosa. I dove out of the way and just barely avoided being trampled. The last thing I saw before hitting the ground was the crazed look in Tank's eyes.

I only had one choice, and she was eyeing me with disdain, but what could I do? I grabbed a bridle from the tack room and approached her carefully, talking in what I hoped were soothing tones.

"Come on, girl," I whispered encouragingly.

I slipped the bit into her mouth and quickly slid the bridle over her ears, buckling the leather strap beneath her neck. There was no time for a saddle. Before she could protest, I leaped onto her back and dug in with my heels. She immediately reared up, trying to knock me off.

"Not now," I said, patting her neck with one hand, tightening the reins with the other. She snorted belligerently and I could tell she was thinking about bucking. I wasn't sure I could hang on if she did.

I leaned forward, made a clicking noise with my tongue and gave her a mighty kick. To my relief, she shot forward.

Tank was already far ahead of me, but I knew from experience that I had the faster horse. Of course, I also had the orneriest mustang that ever lived.

But to my surprise, she was responding well to my commands. I'd never ridden her bareback before. She seemed to prefer it to the saddle.

The Appaloosa turned east, heading for the thick forest surrounding the ranch. From the look of it, Tank was a fairly good rider. I kicked the mustang harder, willing her to catch up. If he made it into the forest, he could easily disappear. And ambush me, I thought, glad I at least had the .38 in my shoulder holster.

Sure enough, as I rounded the bend, I saw the hind end of the Appaloosa vanish into a thick stand of evergreens. I had no choice, really. I pushed the mustang onward.

When we got to the trees, I had a decision to make. Had he taken the trail that led north, or picked his way through the trees straight ahead? I pulled my horse to a stop and tried to listen, but her breathing and my own thumping heart were all I could hear.

I studied the ground. The recent storm had not only washed away whatever tracks had been left from earlier trail rides, but the earth was damp enough for the Appaloosa's hooves to leave distinct impressions. To my relief, Tank had taken the horse-trail.

I took off at a slow lope, keeping my eyes glued to the ground, watching the hoof prints. If they suddenly stopped, I'd know I was in trouble.

But Tank was heading due north, and I wondered if he knew that this trail would lead him straight back to the front of Booker's ranch, once it curved around to the west. Back to where Rosie was waiting for Booker on the front porch, I thought. It would also take him out to the main road, where he'd probably parked his car. If all he wanted to do was to get away, maybe I should just let him go. But what if he was circling back around with the intent of finishing off Rosie? The look in his eyes had told me he was crazy enough to try just that.

Throwing caution to the wind, I kicked the mustang's flanks, urging her to go even faster. It was hard riding, but we'd been on this trail before and she knew it well. She flew over the ground while I hugged her neck, dodging tree limbs and sending silent prayers skyward.

Suddenly, I saw him up ahead. He was taking it

more cautiously than I was and I'd gained quite a lot of ground. But when he turned around and saw me, he kicked the Appaloosa into action.

Even so, I continued to gain on him. He was only a dozen yards away from me, when I realized we were about to come to the edge of the ranch. Unfortunately, the ranch was defined by the same five-foot fence that the mustang had refused to jump only a week earlier. By the way he was slowing, I could tell Tank was as nervous about jumping the fence as I was.

I could shoot him now, I thought, sliding the gun out of the holster. But Tank had made up his mind and was heading practically full-speed toward the fence. I followed, willing the mustang, for once in her measly life, to do the right thing.

The Appaloosa coiled her muscles and leaped over the fence as if he were made to jump. I felt the mustang tense her muscles too, her rear end twitching, her ears laid back with determination.

"Come on, baby, you can do it this time," I murmured.

I readied myself for the graceful leap. I could almost feel myself gliding over the fence. And then, like the rotten animal she was, she not only put on the brakes, she gave what had to be the mightiest buck in equine history and sent me whizzing through the air like a slingshot.

I was airborne, the gun clutched in my right hand, somersaulting through nothingness ten feet above the ground at what felt like sixty miles an hour. When I realized what was about to happen, I acted on pure instinct.

The Appaloosa, having cleared the fence, pulled up

hobbling. Tank had turned to look back and when he saw me hurtling over the fence, he tried to dodge me. He didn't stand a chance. My feet slammed into his chest and we both tumbled hard onto the ground.

When I rolled, the gun hit the ground and went off, causing both horses to bolt. Tank was on top of me immediately, his hand prying the gun loose from the same hand his father had nearly broken. My wrist was no match for his strength, and before I knew it, Tank was standing over me, the gun aimed straight at my head.

We were both out of breath. I sat up slowly, ignoring the gun as best I could, rubbing my damaged wrist.

"Just tell me why, Tank," I said, hoping if I stalled him long enough, Booker would follow the gunshot. He backed up a bit but kept the gun leveled at my eyes. Then he laughed, a short ugly bark that sent chills right through me.

"Why I set up my old man? Because I hate his guts, that's why."

"I meant the women, Tank. Why did you do that to all those women?"

"It isn't what you told all those people," he spat. His eyes had taken on a demented, crazed look. It was difficult to believe I'd never seen this side of him before. "You told people I was a cross dresser. A faggot. That's not true. Fags love men. I just hate women." He seemed inanely proud of this sentiment.

"But why, Tank? I don't get it."

Actually, I thought I did, but I needed to buy time. I tried to stand up, but he waved the gun at me and took aim.

"Every one of those women I visited," he said,

punctuating each syllable, "they were my dear sweet mother, Lila. Poor, sweet Lila, who wouldn't lift a finger to stop her husband, a six-foot, two-hundred-pound man, from beating a six-year-old boy. Her son! Because what would the neighbors think? And you know what?" His voice had become high-pitched, verging on hysteria. "You know what?" he demanded.

I shook my head obediently.

"Every single one of those women were just the same. Never told a soul. Afraid of what the neighbors would think! They were all, every one of them, just like my mother!" He had begun to sob noisily, his shoulders heaving with the effort. But no tears fell from his shiny, crazed eyes.

"It was wrong what happened to you, but it was wrong what you did."

"Oh, please, Cass. Don't start giving me a moral sermon. It's a little late for that, don't you think?" He was gulping air, fighting for breath. "The last thing I need from you is the third degree. I got enough of that from my father to last me a lifetime." His whole body was wracked with the tearless sobs, and even from a foot away, I could smell the sour body odor that so many of the women had reported. The difference was, he hadn't used his dad's Old Spice to cover it up this time. That game was over. I noticed the gun in his hand was jerking as he sobbed.

"Give me the gun, Tank," I said softly.

"Oh, no. Not this time. This time I'm going to do what I set out to do."

"You need help."

"I needed help twenty-two years ago. It's too late for help now."

To my amazement, despite his shaking, he started to laugh.

"What?" I asked. Where in the hell was Booker, anyway?

"You know Tommy Greene?" he asked. I nodded, wondering at the change in his demeanor.

"You know this new kick he's on? Random Acts of Kindness?"

Again I nodded, wondering where this was going.

"Well, consider this one of those."

Tank raised the gun so that it was pointed squarely between my eyes. His mouth opened wide, as if he were suddenly surprised by what he was about to do, and then, raising the gun to his own lips, he pulled the trigger.

Chapter Twenty-three

The boat floated gently on the water, hardly making a ripple. We were lying side by side on the bow cushions, holding hands. The sun beat down, warming us, browning our skin. Every now and then a fish jumped or an osprey dove, but other than that, the cove was undisturbed.

"Look!" she said, pointing to a doe and her fawn drinking at the bank.

"Come here," I said.

"You always get so bossy," she teased, sliding over.

"This isn't bossy. This is passionate."

"Oh. Well, it's been a while. How was I supposed to know?"

I smothered her last comment with my lips, feeling her feigned resistance melt. After a while, she moved away.

"Sooner or later, we're going to have to talk," she said, caressing my knee with soft hands.

My stomach tightened and I felt my hands clamp. Consciously, I unclenched them. "There's really not that much to say."

"You do still love her, though."

I nodded, my mouth suddenly dry.

"But you chose me. Do you even know why?"

An osprey dove, splashing cool water across our legs.

"I love you more."

"How can you be sure?" she asked. She was leaning up on an elbow, peering at me intently. Her eyes were emeralds, forcing me to meet her gaze.

"Because," I said, "I may have wanted to go to bed with Erica. But I realized it was only you I wanted to wake up with."

Maggie smiled, a smile I'd wanted to see for a long, long time.

A few of the publications of
THE NAIAD PRESS, INC.
P.O. Box 10543 • Tallahassee, Florida 32302
Phone (850) 539-5965
Toll-Free Order Number: 1-800-533-1973
Mail orders welcome. Please include 15% postage.
Write or call for our free catalog which also features an
incredible selection of lesbian videos.

SEA TO SHINING SEA by Lisa Shapiro. 256 pp. Unable to resist the raging passion . . . ISBN 1-56280-177-5 $11.95

THIRD DEGREE by Kate Calloway. 224 pp. 3rd Cassidy James mystery. ISBN 1-56280-185-6   11.95

WHEN THE DANCING STOPS by Therese Szymanski. 272 pp. 1st Brett Higgins mystery. ISBN 1-56280-186-4   11.95

PHASES OF THE MOON by Julia Watts. 192 pp. . . . . hungry for everything life has to offer. ISBN 1-56280-176-7   11.95

BABY IT'S COLD by Jaye Maiman. 256 pp. 5th Robin Miller mystery. ISBN 1-56280-156-2   10.95

CLASS REUNION by Linda Hill. 176 pp. The girl from her past . . . ISBN 1-56280-178-3   11.95

DREAM LOVER by Lyn Denison. 224 pp. A soft, sensuous, romantic fantasy. ISBN 1-56280-173-1   11.95

FORTY LOVE by Diana Simmonds. 288 pp. Joyous, heart-warming romance. ISBN 1-56280-171-6   11.95

IN THE MOOD by Robbi Sommers. 160 pp. The queen of erotic tension! ISBN 1-56280-172-4   11.95

SWIMMING CAT COVE by Lauren Douglas. 192 pp. 2nd Allison O'Neil Mystery. ISBN 1-56280-168-6   11.95

THE LOVING LESBIAN by Claire McNab and Sharon Gedan. 240 pp. Explore the experiences that make lesbian love unique. ISBN 1-56280-169-4   14.95

COURTED by Celia Cohen. 160 pp. Sparkling romantic encounter. ISBN 1-56280-166-X   11.95

SEASONS OF THE HEART by Jackie Calhoun. 240 pp. Romance through the years. ISBN 1-56280-167-8   11.95

K. C. BOMBER by Janet McClellan. 208 pp. 1st Tru North mystery. ISBN 1-56280-157-0   11.95

LAST RITES by Tracey Richardson. 192 pp. 1st Stevie Houston mystery. ISBN 1-56280-164-3   11.95

EMBRACE IN MOTION by Karin Kallmaker. 256 pp. A whirlwind love affair. ISBN 1-56280-165-1   11.95

HOT CHECK by Peggy J. Herring. 192 pp. Will workaholic Alice fall for guitarist Ricky? ISBN 1-56280-163-5   11.95

OLD TIES by Saxon Bennett. 176 pp. Can Cleo surrender to a passionate new love? ISBN 1-56280-159-7   11.95

LOVE ON THE LINE by Laura DeHart Young. 176 pp. Will Stef win Kay's heart? ISBN 1-56280-162-7   11.95

DEVIL'S LEG CROSSING by Kaye Davis. 192 pp. 1st Maris Middleton mystery. ISBN 1-56280-158-9   11.95

COSTA BRAVA by Marta Balletbo Coll. 144 pp. Read the book, see the movie! ISBN 1-56280-153-8   11.95

MEETING MAGDALENE & OTHER STORIES by Marilyn Freeman. 144 pp. Read the book, see the movie! ISBN 1-56280-170-8   11.95

SECOND FIDDLE by Kate Calloway. 208 pp. P.I. Cassidy James' second case. ISBN 1-56280-169-6   11.95

LAUREL by Isabel Miller. 128 pp. By the author of the beloved *Patience and Sarah.* ISBN 1-56280-146-5   10.95

LOVE OR MONEY by Jackie Calhoun. 240 pp. The romance of real life. ISBN 1-56280-147-3   10.95

SMOKE AND MIRRORS by Pat Welch. 224 pp. 5th Helen Black Mystery. ISBN 1-56280-143-0   10.95

DANCING IN THE DARK edited by Barbara Grier & Christine Cassidy. 272 pp. Erotic love stories by Naiad Press authors. ISBN 1-56280-144-9   14.95

TIME AND TIME AGAIN by Catherine Ennis. 176 pp. Passionate love affair. ISBN 1-56280-145-7   10.95

PAXTON COURT by Diane Salvatore. 256 pp. Erotic and wickedly funny contemporary tale about the business of learning to live together. ISBN 1-56280-114-7   10.95

INNER CIRCLE by Claire McNab. 208 pp. 8th Carol Ashton Mystery. ISBN 1-56280-135-X   11.95

LESBIAN SEX: AN ORAL HISTORY by Susan Johnson. 240 pp. Need we say more? ISBN 1-56280-142-2   14.95

WILD THINGS by Karin Kallmaker. 240 pp. By the undisputed mistress of lesbian romance. ISBN 1-56280-139-2   11.95

THE GIRL NEXT DOOR by Mindy Kaplan. 208 pp. Just what you'd expect. ISBN 1-56280-140-6   11.95

THE FIRST TIME EVER edited by Barbara Grier & Christine Cassidy. 272 pp. Love stories by Naiad Press authors.
ISBN 1-56280-086-8   14.95

MISS PETTIBONE AND MISS McGRAW by Brenda Weathers. 208 pp. A charming ghostly love story.   ISBN 1-56280-151-1   10.95

CHANGES by Jackie Calhoun. 208 pp. Involved romance and relationships.   ISBN 1-56280-083-3   10.95

FAIR PLAY by Rose Beecham. 256 pp. 3rd Amanda Valentine Mystery.   ISBN 1-56280-081-7   10.95

PAYBACK by Celia Cohen. 176 pp. A gripping thriller of romance, revenge and betrayal.   ISBN 1-56280-084-1   10.95

THE BEACH AFFAIR by Barbara Johnson. 224 pp. Sizzling summer romance/mystery/intrigue.   ISBN 1-56280-090-6   10.95

GETTING THERE by Robbi Sommers. 192 pp. Nobody does it like Robbi!   ISBN 1-56280-099-X   10.95

FINAL CUT by Lisa Haddock. 208 pp. 2nd Carmen Ramirez Mystery.   ISBN 1-56280-088-4   10.95

FLASHPOINT by Katherine V. Forrest. 256 pp. A Lesbian blockbuster!   ISBN 1-56280-079-5   10.95

CLAIRE OF THE MOON by Nicole Conn. Audio Book —Read by Marianne Hyatt.   ISBN 1-56280-113-9   16.95

FOR LOVE AND FOR LIFE: INTIMATE PORTRAITS OF LESBIAN COUPLES by Susan Johnson. 224 pp.
ISBN 1-56280-091-4   14.95

DEVOTION by Mindy Kaplan. 192 pp. See the movie — read the book!   ISBN 1-56280-093-0   10.95

SOMEONE TO WATCH by Jaye Maiman. 272 pp. 4th Robin Miller Mystery.   ISBN 1-56280-095-7   10.95

GREENER THAN GRASS by Jennifer Fulton. 208 pp. A young woman — a stranger in her bed.   ISBN 1-56280-092-2   10.95

TRAVELS WITH DIANA HUNTER by Regine Sands. Erotic lesbian romp. Audio Book (2 cassettes)   ISBN 1-56280-107-4   16.95

CABIN FEVER by Carol Schmidt. 256 pp. Sizzling suspense and passion.   ISBN 1-56280-089-1   10.95

THERE WILL BE NO GOODBYES by Laura DeHart Young. 192 pp. Romantic love, strength, and friendship.   ISBN 1-56280-103-1   10.95

FAULTLINE by Sheila Ortiz Taylor. 144 pp. Joyous comic lesbian novel.   ISBN 1-56280-108-2   9.95

OPEN HOUSE by Pat Welch. 176 pp. 4th Helen Black Mystery.
ISBN 1-56280-102-3   10.95

ONCE MORE WITH FEELING by Peggy J. Herring. 240 pp. Lighthearted, loving romantic adventure.   ISBN 1-56280-089-2   10.95

FOREVER by Evelyn Kennedy. 224 pp. Passionate romance — love overcoming all obstacles. ISBN 1-56280-094-9   10.95

WHISPERS by Kris Bruyer. 176 pp. Romantic ghost story ISBN 1-56280-082-5   10.95

NIGHT SONGS by Penny Mickelbury. 224 pp. 2nd Gianna Maglione Mystery. ISBN 1-56280-097-3   10.95

GETTING TO THE POINT by Teresa Stores. 256 pp. Classic southern Lesbian novel. ISBN 1-56280-100-7   10.95

PAINTED MOON by Karin Kallmaker. 224 pp. Delicious Kallmaker romance. ISBN 1-56280-075-2   11.95

THE MYSTERIOUS NAIAD edited by Katherine V. Forrest & Barbara Grier. 320 pp. Love stories by Naiad Press authors. ISBN 1-56280-074-4   14.95

DAUGHTERS OF A CORAL DAWN by Katherine V. Forrest. 240 pp. Tenth Anniversay Edition. ISBN 1-56280-104-X   11.95

BODY GUARD by Claire McNab. 208 pp. 6th Carol Ashton Mystery. ISBN 1-56280-073-6   11.95

CACTUS LOVE by Lee Lynch. 192 pp. Stories by the beloved storyteller. ISBN 1-56280-071-X   9.95

SECOND GUESS by Rose Beecham. 216 pp. 2nd Amanda Valentine Mystery. ISBN 1-56280-069-8   9.95

A RAGE OF MAIDENS by Lauren Wright Douglas. 240 pp. 6th Caitlin Reece Mystery. ISBN 1-56280-068-X   10.95

TRIPLE EXPOSURE by Jackie Calhoun. 224 pp. Romantic drama involving many characters. ISBN 1-56280-067-1   10.95

UP, UP AND AWAY by Catherine Ennis. 192 pp. Delightful romance. ISBN 1-56280-065-5   11.95

PERSONAL ADS by Robbi Sommers. 176 pp. Sizzling short stories. ISBN 1-56280-059-0   11.95

CROSSWORDS by Penny Sumner. 256 pp. 2nd Victoria Cross Mystery. ISBN 1-56280-064-7   9.95

SWEET CHERRY WINE by Carol Schmidt. 224 pp. A novel of suspense. ISBN 1-56280-063-9   9.95

CERTAIN SMILES by Dorothy Tell. 160 pp. Erotic short stories. ISBN 1-56280-066-3   9.95

EDITED OUT by Lisa Haddock. 224 pp. 1st Carmen Ramirez Mystery. ISBN 1-56280-077-9   9.95

WEDNESDAY NIGHTS by Camarin Grae. 288 pp. Sexy adventure. ISBN 1-56280-060-4   10.95

SMOKEY O by Celia Cohen. 176 pp. Relationships on the playing field. ISBN 1-56280-057-4   9.95

KATHLEEN O'DONALD by Penny Hayes. 256 pp. Rose and
Kathleen find each other and employment in 1909 NYC.
ISBN 1-56280-070-1   9.95

STAYING HOME by Elisabeth Nonas. 256 pp. Molly and Alix
want a baby . . . or do they?   ISBN 1-56280-076-0   10.95

TRUE LOVE by Jennifer Fulton. 240 pp. Six lesbians searching
for love in all the "right" places.   ISBN 1-56280-035-3   10.95

KEEPING SECRETS by Penny Mickelbury. 208 pp. 1st Gianna
Maglione Mystery.   ISBN 1-56280-052-3   9.95

THE ROMANTIC NAIAD edited by Katherine V. Forrest &
Barbara Grier. 336 pp. Love stories by Naiad Press authors.
ISBN 1-56280-054-X   14.95

UNDER MY SKIN by Jaye Maiman. 336 pp. 3rd Robin Miller
Mystery.   ISBN 1-56280-049-3.   11.95

CAR POOL by Karin Kallmaker. 272pp. Lesbians on wheels
and then some!   ISBN 1-56280-048-5   10.95

NOT TELLING MOTHER: STORIES FROM A LIFE by Diane
Salvatore. 176 pp. Her 3rd novel.   ISBN 1-56280-044-2   9.95

GOBLIN MARKET by Lauren Wright Douglas. 240pp. 5th Caitlin
Reece Mystery.   ISBN 1-56280-047-7   10.95

LONG GOODBYES by Nikki Baker. 256 pp. 3rd Virginia Kelly
Mystery.   ISBN 1-56280-042-6   9.95

FRIENDS AND LOVERS by Jackie Calhoun. 224 pp. Mid-
western Lesbian lives and loves.   ISBN 1-56280-041-8   11.95

BEHIND CLOSED DOORS by Robbi Sommers. 192 pp. Hot,
erotic short stories.   ISBN 1-56280-039-6   11.95

CLAIRE OF THE MOON by Nicole Conn. 192 pp. See the
movie — read the book!   ISBN 1-56280-038-8   10.95

SILENT HEART by Claire McNab. 192 pp. Exotic Lesbian
romance.   ISBN 1-56280-036-1   10.95

THE SPY IN QUESTION by Amanda Kyle Williams. 256 pp.
4th Madison McGuire Mystery.   ISBN 1-56280-037-X   9.95

SAVING GRACE by Jennifer Fulton. 240 pp. Adventure and
romantic entanglement.   ISBN 1-56280-051-5   10.95

CURIOUS WINE by Katherine V. Forrest. 176 pp. Tenth Anniver-
sary Edition. The most popular contemporary Lesbian love story.
ISBN 1-56280-053-1   11.95
    Audio Book (2 cassettes)   ISBN 1-56280-105-8   16.95

CHAUTAUQUA by Catherine Ennis. 192 pp. Exciting, romantic
adventure.   ISBN 1-56280-032-9   9.95

A PROPER BURIAL by Pat Welch. 192 pp. 3rd Helen Black
Mystery.   ISBN 1-56280-033-7   9.95

STILL WATERS by Pat Welch. 208 pp. 2nd Helen Black Mystery.
ISBN 0-941483-97-5   9.95

TO LOVE AGAIN by Evelyn Kennedy. 208 pp. Wildly romantic
love story.   ISBN 0-941483-85-1   11.95

IN THE GAME by Nikki Baker. 192 pp. 1st Virginia Kelly
Mystery.   ISBN 1-56280-004-3   9.95

STRANDED by Camarin Grae. 320 pp. Entertaining, riveting
adventure.   ISBN 0-941483-99-1   9.95

THE DAUGHTERS OF ARTEMIS by Lauren Wright Douglas.
240 pp. 3rd Caitlin Reece Mystery.   ISBN 0-941483-95-9   9.95

CLEARWATER by Catherine Ennis. 176 pp. Romantic secrets
of a small Louisiana town.   ISBN 0-941483-65-7   8.95

THE HALLELUJAH MURDERS by Dorothy Tell. 176 pp. 2nd
Poppy Dillworth Mystery.   ISBN 0-941483-88-6   8.95

SECOND CHANCE by Jackie Calhoun. 256 pp. Contemporary
Lesbian lives and loves.   ISBN 0-941483-93-2   9.95

BENEDICTION by Diane Salvatore. 272 pp. Striking, contemporary romantic novel.   ISBN 0-941483-90-8   11.95

TOUCHWOOD by Karin Kallmaker. 240 pp. Loving, May/
December romance.   ISBN 0-941483-76-2   11.95

COP OUT by Claire McNab. 208 pp. 4th Carol Ashton Mystery.
ISBN 0-941483-84-3   10.95

THE BEVERLY MALIBU by Katherine V. Forrest. 288 pp. 3rd
Kate Delafield Mystery.   ISBN 0-941483-48-7   11.95

THE PROVIDENCE FILE by Amanda Kyle Williams. 256 pp.
2nd Madison McGuire Mystery.   ISBN 0-941483-92-4   8.95

I LEFT MY HEART by Jaye Maiman. 320 pp. 1st Robin Miller
Mystery.   ISBN 0-941483-72-X   11.95

THE PRICE OF SALT by Patricia Highsmith (writing as Claire
Morgan). 288 pp. Classic lesbian novel, first issued in 1952 . . .
acknowledged by its author under her own, very famous, name.
ISBN 1-56280-003-5   10.95

SIDE BY SIDE by Isabel Miller. 256 pp. From beloved author of
Patience and Sarah.   ISBN 0-941483-77-0   10.95

STAYING POWER: LONG TERM LESBIAN COUPLES by
Susan E. Johnson. 352 pp. Joys of coupledom. ISBN 0-941-483-75-4   14.95

SLICK by Camarin Grae. 304 pp. Exotic, erotic adventure.
ISBN 0-941483-74-6   9.95

NINTH LIFE by Lauren Wright Douglas. 256 pp. 2nd Caitlin
Reece Mystery.   ISBN 0-941483-50-9   9.95

PLAYERS by Robbi Sommers. 192 pp. Sizzling, erotic novel.
ISBN 0-941483-73-8   9.95

MURDER AT RED ROOK RANCH by Dorothy Tell. 224 pp.
1st Poppy Dillworth Mystery.   ISBN 0-941483-80-0   8.95

A ROOM FULL OF WOMEN by Elisabeth Nonas. 256 pp.
Contemporary Lesbian lives.   ISBN 0-941483-69-X   9.95

THEME FOR DIVERSE INSTRUMENTS by Jane Rule. 208 pp.
Powerful romantic lesbian stories.   ISBN 0-941483-63-0   8.95

CLUB 12 by Amanda Kyle Williams. 288 pp. Espionage thriller
featuring a lesbian agent!   ISBN 0-941483-64-9   9.95

DEATH DOWN UNDER by Claire McNab. 240 pp. 3rd Carol
Ashton Mystery.   ISBN 0-941483-39-8   10.95

MONTANA FEATHERS by Penny Hayes. 256 pp. Vivian and
Elizabeth find love in frontier Montana.   ISBN 0-941483-61-4   9.95

LIFESTYLES by Jackie Calhoun. 224 pp. Contemporary Lesbian
lives and loves.   ISBN 0-941483-57-6   10.95

MURDER BY THE BOOK by Pat Welch. 256 pp. 1st Helen
Black Mystery.   ISBN 0-941483-59-2   9.95

THERE'S SOMETHING I'VE BEEN MEANING TO TELL YOU
Ed. by Loralee MacPike. 288 pp. Gay men and lesbians coming out
to their children.   ISBN 0-941483-44-4   9.95

LIFTING BELLY by Gertrude Stein. Ed. by Rebecca Mark. 104 pp.
Erotic poetry.   ISBN 0-941483-51-7   10.95

AFTER THE FIRE by Jane Rule. 256 pp. Warm, human novel by
this incomparable author.   ISBN 0-941483-45-2   8.95

PLEASURES by Robbi Sommers. 204 pp. Unprecedented
eroticism.   ISBN 0-941483-49-5   11.95

EDGEWISE by Camarin Grae. 372 pp. Spellbinding
adventure.   ISBN 0-941483-19-3   9.95

FATAL REUNION by Claire McNab. 224 pp. 2nd Carol Ashton
Mystery.   ISBN 0-941483-40-1   10.95

IN EVERY PORT by Karin Kallmaker. 228 pp. Jessica's sexy,
adventuresome travels.   ISBN 0-941483-37-7   10.95

OF LOVE AND GLORY by Evelyn Kennedy. 192 pp. Exciting
WWII romance.   ISBN 0-941483-32-0   10.95

CLICKING STONES by Nancy Tyler Glenn. 288 pp. Love
transcending time.   ISBN 0-941483-31-2   9.95

These are just a few of the many Naiad Press titles — we are the oldest and
largest lesbian/feminist publishing company in the world. We also offer an
enormous selection of lesbian video products. Please request a complete
catalog. We offer personal service; we encourage and welcome direct mail
orders from individuals who have limited access to bookstores carrying our
publications.